DEFIER

THE GIRL WHO STOOD

MANDY FENDER

Book Cover Design: Paper and Sage Design
Bird Cover Art: Shutterstock @Grafikwork
Girl Cover Photo: Shutterstock @Aleshyn_Andrei
Lion Vector: Designed by Freepik
Formatting: Polgarus Studio

ISBN-13: 978-0692475003
ISBN-10: 0692475001

Stouthearted Publishing

DEDICATION

This book is dedicated to all of the brave Christians around the world.

1 Thessalonians 2:2 "…but with the help of our God we dared to tell you his gospel in the face of strong opposition."

May you continue to be brave and dare to fight for your faith.

"Be strong and courageous. Do not be afraid or terrified because of them, for the LORD your God goes with you; he will never leave you nor forsake you."

Deuteronomy 31:6

Chapter 1

The funeral home's stretch limo halted in Lennox's driveway, causing her to sway forward as it stopped. Raindrops clicked against the metal roof above her. Looking out the front window, she blinked away tears that stung her eyes. Her home stood before her as a reminder of what she would never have again, an empty shell of what used to be.

The once vibrant flowers her mom planted in the window boxes already seemed to wither away. The spring rains of late March weighed heavily on the tree's leaves. The light blue paint chipped off the shutters and the white wood panels were full of rot. She wondered why she never noticed them before. It was as if her senses muted the beauty and replaced it with sorrow.

At the age of seventeen, it was hard for Lennox to fully process the emotions that came with losing her parents the week before. Oliver—her brother—sat beside her. His fingers tapped against the tan leather of the back seat. He chewed on his cheek and shook his head like when he was young so he wouldn't cry. He was the older of the two at age twenty, and Oliver tried to be strong for the both of them. He had put his life on hold with the horrific news of their parents' deaths and left college so he could take care of her. His dreams of becoming an engineer would wait a little longer.

Lennox tuned out the voices in her head and focused on the pain in her soul. There would be no more family game nights, no more family birthday celebrations. Her mom and dad would never be with them again.

Something in her soul snapped hard and fast. She couldn't do this. It was too much all at once. She couldn't take any more tearful condolences or stare into any more solemn faces. Most of all, Lennox couldn't take the unknown. The coroner ruled her parents' deaths a double homicide, but local authorities had no leads on who committed the crime, or why. It was the unknown that forced Lennox to be irrational. Even with the funeral over, she felt no closure and had no peace.

Men and women dressed in black, held umbrellas and lined the curved sidewalk with casserole dishes in their hands, waiting for the two of them to get out of the vehicle. As tissues dabbed at their eyes, tears swelled in Lennox's eyes.

No! I can't do this.

She bolted from the limo and headed to the abandoned silo where her dad took her when she was little. It was where she always felt safe and where the world once made sense.

The men and women on the sidewalk watched with low murmurs of concern as Lennox fled. Eyebrows raised and shoulders collapsed as she ran far away from them. Her troubled mind registered the looks. It occurred to her she was a colossal disappointment for choosing not to stay. On some level, Lennox was disappointed in herself. She should have greeted her guests at least, but her need for privacy overrode her sense of duty.

Somewhere behind her amidst all the things she could not deal with, Oliver swung open the limo door and chased after her. The sight of him took her back to feelings of when they were kids who played out in the rain. She would jump in puddles as he chased after her with mud in his hands. She wanted to return to those safe days of innocence and ignorance.

When he caught up to her, he grabbed her wrist and spun her around. The rain plastered his dirty blond hair on his face as his hazel eyes stared into hers. His eyes were so similar to her own. He pleaded silently with her, asking her to not run away from everything. She placed her hand on top of his and looked at his stoic face with sadness. She disappointed him as well.

"I'm sorry, please forgive me," she said with a vice around her heart that squeezed her chest so tight it felt like it would explode.

His hand loosened from her wrist and fell back to his side. Instead of scolding his sister, Oliver pulled her into a tight embrace. "One day at a time," he whispered into her hair.

"One day at a time" was the Winters' family mantra for as long as Lennox could remember. When Oliver or Lennox had a difficult time with anything—especially school—they counted on their parents and each other to give that encouragement. Their parents were never overtly hard on them, but rather encouraged them to hold their heads up high and learn from every part of life they went through—good or bad.

"I can't. I just can't," Lennox said, readying her feet to run again. Oliver said nothing more as he watched her turn and head back down the road, leaving him behind to deal with the mourners. Fear, anger, and confusion made her become someone she did not want to be. She felt bad for leaving him there, but she had to get away.

The black funeral dress she wore stunted her stride. The lace trim frayed like her heart. Its delicate stitching unraveled and scratched her skin as she moved. The drops of rain washed the tears from her cheeks until she couldn't tell the difference between them. The straps of her high heels slid from her ankles, making it even harder to run.

Blasted heels.

Fighting everything in and around her, Lennox kicked them away, not caring where they landed. They flew into Mr. Urchin's finely pruned hedges. He could throw them away if he wanted to. Her feet slapped the sidewalk with every stride and splashed warm water to her knees. Her lungs begged her to stop and her feet screamed to slow down. As the world fell apart before her eyes, her heart pounded out the truth that life was an unfair tragedy she could not escape.

After what seemed like miles of running, she reached the silo. The long stretch of pavement stopped and turned into a road of mud. Fields of blooming cotton surrounded her. The sea of white fluff, reduced to a wide strip around the silo, reminded her of billowing clouds in the aftermath of a storm.

Trying to catch her breath, she stared at the dilapidated red barn that rested twenty feet away. It resembled how she felt on the inside. At one time, that barn was full of life and purpose, but now it was nothing except run down and useless. This small, God-fearing Texas town was turned upside down, and she was turned upside down right along with it.

She climbed the silo's ladder. Her feet slipped against the damp rungs as she goes higher and higher. Pushing herself over the last rung and up onto the top of the silo, she fell to her knees. She took a deep breath and screamed at the top of her lungs to release everything that was building up inside, but to no avail. Her sorrow would not let go of her.

The rain quieted to a drizzle and tiny beads of water rested on Lennox's skin as she pulled her hands up over her arms. She looked out over the city from the height of the silo and stood to her feet. Her toes stopped at the ledge of the silo's roof as her hands wrapped around the rails. She held her breath for a moment and then let it free. As she stood there, watching the upside down world spread before her, she determined to make sense of the pieces of the puzzle that were missing. Living without answers made her desperate for the truth. She did not understand why God would let this happen. None of it made any sense to her. Her parents did not deserve to die. She did not deserve to lose them. Life was too fragile and flesh was too frail.

Her father's words again rang in her ears. "Tomorrow is not promised to anyone. That is why you must live every day like it's your last."

If only she could go back and stop it all from happening, but there was nothing she could do to turn back the hands of time. Nothing she could change to make it right. She blinked several more tears away and felt heaviness in her heart. Nothing would ever be the same.

Her dad's gentle voice rippled in her thoughts. She could hear him tell her that one day, she could be like one of the people in his stories who changed the world. He said it with so much conviction that he almost made her believe him, but she could not even live in her own world anymore. Let alone change it. Her heart searched for escape from the ache as anger churned inside her soul like acid and corroded any faith she had left.

The sun broke through the clouds above her, cascading its light onto the houses in the distance. The cotton fields turned white as snow from the glare. The light drew her closer to its warmth. She sat on top of the silo and wrapped her arms around her legs with her head cradled to her knees. A thousand questions floated in her brain. She picked out the one she needed answered most.

God, where are you?

Chapter 2

One Month Later…

Lennox squinted and saw the neon green light flash on her clock through her eyelashes. It read 5 a.m. Once again, she woke up before her alarm sounded. Getting up with the sun was Lennox's new normal. Since she still had nightmares about her parents' deaths, even waking up too early seemed worthwhile.

Lennox's one-hundred-pound German shepherd, Grizzly, nuzzled her way through the cracked door and sat down beside Lennox's bed. Grizzly looked like any other German shepherd, except for the patch of white fur on her chin. Grizz was a retired police dog that Lennox begged for. There was just something special about her, and Lennox had to have her.

Rolling the covers away from her body, Lennox sat on the edge of the bed and hesitated to move. Grizzly nudged Lennox's knee with her nose and Lennox gave her a small pat on the head as she decided to leave her room.

The floor creaked under Lennox's feet as she opened the bathroom door. Leaning against the pedestal sink, she splashed water on her face and ignored putting on any makeup. She sighed. Makeup was not enough to hide her restless nights. The truth that she still struggled to sleep could not be covered. She was a mess, but somehow she managed to fix her hair and get into clothes that weren't too wrinkled. It was a start.

Staring at herself in the foggy mirror, she took a towel and wiped away the condensation that faded her reflection. Returning to school was one of the hardest steps for Lennox. Senior year was supposed to be one of the best years of her life, but now everyone looked at her with pity in their eyes. They did not know how to act in her presence. She wouldn't know how to act either if she were them.

"Another week. You can do this." She stared at her reflection. The hazel eyes staring back at her were not as tired as the morning before, but still a little puffy. Compared to the first week of school, week two was already looking brighter for Lennox. Maybe she was getting her act together more than she realized.

"Lennox, time for school!" Oliver yelled from downstairs.

"Coming!" she shouted back, looking one last time in her full-length mirror. Her faded jeans were tucked into her boots, and her gray shirt was disheveled and too big. It didn't matter. She quickly gathered her hair in her hands and tied it back into a high ponytail.

The smell of blueberry muffins wafted through the air. Oliver had a plate of them and a cup of orange juice waiting for Lennox on the kitchen table. Instead of his typical shorts and semi-wrinkly polo, Oliver was dressed in khaki pants with a crisp, blue button up shirt that was tucked in.

"Why are you all dressed up?" Lennox asked with raised eyebrows.

"I have a job interview today. I have to figure out a way to keep us in this house."

"Oh." Lennox missed the days when mornings were carefree. Everything took such a serious turn. "Good luck."

"Thanks, but I don't need luck. God's got it," he said full of confidence. It seemed that his faith never wavered and she wondered how he could so easily trust God after everything that had happened.

"You ready to go?" Lennox asked, looking at her watch and ignoring the reference to God.

She still had doubts about God, which concerned Oliver. Lennox wanted to avoid getting into another lengthy discussion about it. She wanted to believe in God, but she had major problems and she wanted answers in a major way. She needed to understand why her parents were dead and why God did not intervene. Lennox needed an answer from God to decide how she felt about Him. The real problem was, Lennox was not entirely convinced that God answered prayers—at least not hers.

"Yep, let's go." Oliver walked to the back door with his keys dangling in his hand.

Lennox grabbed her satchel, the one that used to belong to her dad. He used it for work every day as a teacher. It was one of the last things he ever gave her. It was well worn. The brown leather strap was softened almost to suede from years of use. It meant more to Lennox now that he was gone. She wished she had not taken so many things for granted.

She slung the satchel over her shoulder and walked out the back door to the driveway where Oliver's pick-up truck sat. She had walked this path many times before and this time should not be any different, but it was.

At the sight of the black truck, she vividly remembered Oliver turning eighteen and her parents buying it as a graduation surprise for him. Oliver went crazy with excitement. He could not believe it was his. For a split second Lennox smiled at the memory, but then came the heartache. It struck quick and vicious like an unannounced tornado. Lennox wished the memories of her parents did not hurt so much. It felt as if she had an impossible choice: to not think about her parents, or live in constant pain. Neither option was acceptable.

Oliver joined Lennox in the driveway and unlocked the truck. They spent the ten-minute drive to her school in comfortable silence.

"Good luck, again, on your interview," Lennox said as she exited the vehicle. Oliver smiled his goodbye. As he drove away, rolled down his window and yelled "Have a good day!" so loudly that people stopped mid-conversation and turned to look at her.

"Big brothers," she shrugged in explanation. She felt her cheeks grow hot as attention was drawn to her and hurried away from the embarrassing scene.

Lennox's best friends and fellow senior classmates,

Sky and Kira, waited for her on the steps in front of the school building. They smiled at her embarrassment as she walked toward them. Sky sported his typical go-to outfit—a baseball shirt tucked in halfway, blue jeans, and the hunter green cap he always wore backward. He was the star of the high school baseball team and fit the visual role perfectly. Being an athlete in a small Texas town kept him out of trouble… at least, that is what his grandpa always said.

In contrast, petite and fashion forward Kira preferred trendy clothes and always dressed to the nines. She resembled a model in every way but her height. Kira's coral blouse complimented her smooth, tawny complexion. Kira had recently cut off her long dark curls in favor of a pixie cut that showed off her high cheekbones and golden-brown eyes.

Lennox, Sky, and Kira met in kindergarten and were friends ever since. People always called them the unbreakable trio. They were inseparable. One for all and all for one. Sky was very protective of both of them and would keep them safe from bullies during their playground years.

During the hard days and long nights after her parents' deaths, Lennox's friends were always there, even when she attempted to push them away. Sky and Kira were the rocks in her world—a world that was like shifting sand.

Lennox's heart skipped a beat as she saw Sky's welcoming smile. His deep green eyes, muscular six-foot frame, and twin dimples made Lennox melt every time she saw him. Sky was incredibly handsome in her eyes—even in the casual clothes he always wore. She anticipated seeing him all dressed up for their prom, which was just a few weeks away. The trio agreed to forego individual dates and attend together as a unit. Lennox entertained the hope that Sky might ask her to the prom, but at the same time, she was wary of doing anything that might ruin her friendship with him. Adolescent feelings often changed quickly, so Lennox settled comfortably into the "wait-and-see" approach. Maybe one day Sky would discover that he felt romantic attraction for her, but for now, only Kira knew of Lennox's true feelings for Sky.

"Hey, Lennox, you ready for another day?" Kira asked, always concerned with Lennox's well-being. She was the one that Lennox poured her heart out to the most. She would come over and sit on the edge of Lennox's bed and stroke her hair as Lennox sobbed into the pillow.

Kira always knew what to say and always had a word of encouragement.

"I'm okay," Lennox said with a half-hearted smile. She was less talkative and bottled up her words inside so that she would not needlessly lash out at the ones she loved. Words did not come as easily to her anymore.

Sky put his arm around Lennox's shoulder and the three friends entered through the double doors of the school's front entrance. Lennox took a deep breath as they walked through. The archway to the entrance was decorated with hunter green and silver ribbons. For all their festivity, the halls felt like they were closing in on Lennox. They seemed to narrow with every step.

Posters for prom that Lennox was so excited about before covered every inch of spare space on the walls. She already bought her dress with her mom three months ago. Her mother let her spend fifty dollars over the budget. And once again, the memories made her heart hurt. She missed her mom so much.

How drastically life changed and yet, it was still the same. Three months ago Lennox was accessory shopping with her mom without a care in the world. Two months later, her parents were dead. One month after that, she attended school like any other teenager. Lennox took some solace in the fact the initial shell shock of her parents' sudden and still unsolved murders seemed to wear off amongst the student body as a whole. Everyone got their awkward greetings behind them, and almost no one gave Lennox a second glance in the hall anymore. It seemed that life had gone on—at least for everyone else.

The crowd of students slammed lockers shut as they headed to class. The metal crashing into itself made Lennox flinch. Sky pulled her into him to protect her from two boys chasing after each other.

"Thanks." She looked up at Sky, grateful both for his presence and understanding.

His smile reached his eyes. "It's what I'm here for."

Kira gave Lennox an encouraging nod as if to say, "You can do this" as they arrived at their first class— Economics—and took their usual seats in the middle of the room. Their instructor, Mrs. Bradley, maintained her youthful exuberance despite having taught for more than thirty years. She was a favorite among students and faculty. Mrs. Bradley adjusted her red-rimmed glasses and began reviewing a semester's worth of material so the students would know what to study for finals.

Nothing Mrs. Bradley said registered in Lennox's brain, even though Lennox was a straight-A student and

Mrs. Bradley was a skilled teacher. Once an avid note taker, Lennox's notebook was now an empty canvas for words that would not be written. Gone were the days where her main priority was retaining her place in the National Honor Society. Now, she could not bring herself to write anything other than her name over and over again.

Lennox Grace Winters was on the top right-hand corner of the page. Lennox watched the clock click away the time and tapped her pencil with the seconds. The rhythm of the second hand was all she focused on.

Ten seconds… five seconds… one second….

The bell rang and she was on her feet, ready to be distracted from the thoughts that freely roamed her mind without apology.

Kira's short legs rushed to catch up with Lennox who already cleared the doorway and lingered in the hall. As they waited for Sky to finish talking with Mrs. Bradley, Kira excitedly asked Lennox about the prom.

"You're still planning on coming with us to prom, right?"

"Yep, as long as you promise to help me get ready."

"Of course I will."

Lennox, being kind of a tomboy, was okay with doing

makeup and hair, but Kira thrived on it. Lennox would not be surprised if Kira was voted "best dressed" for the yearbook.

Sky walked out of the classroom with an extra credit paper in his hand. "My grandpa insists I make nothing less than a 'B' in this class." He shook his head and strolled down the hall as the girls followed closely behind him.

Lennox faced the rest of the day alone, without the safety net of Sky and Kira. Due to class schedules, they were separated for the remainder of the day.

"See you after school," Kira said as she left Lennox standing in front of her History class.

"Bye guys," Sky said, walking to his own class.

"See you guys later." Lennox watched her rocks disappear.

She took another deep breath and prepared herself for the next class where her mind had time to wander into the abyss of questions that it had become. She could not wait for another day to complete. It meant she was that much closer to summer, when she could search for the answers she so desperately needed—if there were any to be found.

Chapter 3

Lennox curled up on the light yellow couch cushions in her living room and turned on the projector to cloud the thoughts that continually ran rampant. It was tiring to have a mind that refused to rest.

The doorbell rang. Lennox saw the shadows of Sky and Kira through the front door's curtains. She should have known they would come over tonight. They came over as much as they could to support her, even if that just meant sitting in silence.

Lennox opened the door. "Hey guys, come on in."

"My mom made you and Oliver dinner," Kira said, holding up a cream colored ceramic dish. Kira's mom sent them dinner at least twice a week and invited them over every Sunday after church service.

With a grateful heart, Lennox took the dish and set it in the kitchen. She returned to the living room and sat down with her friends who already made themselves at home. Lennox's home was like their second home. Sky rested his head on his left fist. Every now and then, his green eyes would meet Lennox's. Kira gave her a soft, knowing smile and then looked away. The glow of the lamp shone on Kira's skin, making her all the more beautiful.

The projector reflected holograms all around as if they were in the same room with them. The date ran across the top of the light blue walls—April 25, 2030. The reporters appeared and were broadcasting about current events in the states. America was in a fragile position, and the government struggled to keep it together. Then the news turned to a subject matter that hit all too close to home for Lennox.

The police found new evidence in the unsolved homicides of Lennox's parents a month ago. The police chief spoke to Oliver about it, but it was entirely different to see the evidence played out on the news. A terrorist cell released videos of her parents' deaths.

Terror and anger rose in Lennox. She was afraid of what this terrorist cell was capable of and furious at what they had done to her personal little world. They destroyed it forever.

The reporter's voice laid out the facts of the case.

"And we have new information now about the unsolved murders of two locals, Haiden and Cadence Winters, who were murdered just a month ago. Apparently, video has been released from a foreign terrorist cell who calls itself 'The Regime.' The Regime is infamously known to attack Christians and others who oppose their world views."

Lennox's fingernails dug into her palms as she heard what the reporter said. Would she finally have the answer to what really happened, and why? Her parents' pictures popped onto the screen and turned into holograms before them. Their images made her sit straight up on the edge of the couch. She could not look away as she stood up, forgetting she wasn't alone. No one and nothing mattered, except what the projector was playing at that moment.

Mesmerized, Lennox reached toward her parents' holograms, wishing they could reach back. Her hand went right through them, distorting their image. She recoiled. The images reconfigured as she clenched her hands back into fists and rocked back and forth.

Holograms of men whose faces were covered and wore the emblem of a snake coiled around a tree on their sleeves pulled Lennox's parents from the sidewalk and forced them to their knees. She cringed and took a heavy breath. Only a few tears escaped her mom's fair eyes. Her mother's floral dress floated in the air as the wind blew. Her dad fought back the tears that tried to overtake him as he reached for her mother's hand, but the soldiers denied him her touch. Their tears fell. Her dad could no longer fight them from falling. They did not look like tears of fear, but rather tears of sadness. Tears that represented the fact that they knew they would never see Lennox or Oliver again. They knew what was coming, but remained brave. Her parents never wavered. She wished she had half their bravery. She did not understand why they were selected. Was it because they were Christians? If so, how could the Regime know they were?

"Lennox, don't watch this." Oliver jumped up from the kitchen table where he sat eating the meal Kira's mom made and ran to turn off the projection. The images fizzled away as anger rose in Lennox. Her nails dug further into her skin.

"I just want to know why—"

"There is no good reason, is there?" Oliver folded his arms across his chest.

"No, I guess there isn't," Lennox said, relenting to

that horrifically simple understanding.

The tears in her eyes were too big to hold back.

She had to find out why her parents were killed by a terrorist cell. Maybe faith in Christ was too dangerous to hold on to now. Lennox's mind was weary from all of the questions and the fact that they would not let her sleep. Her body ached. She was exhausted from the tossing and turning the nightmares caused every single night. All she wanted was to know *why*. She wiped away her tears with the back of her hand. It was as if her spirit and flesh were in a war zone choosing sides, and both sides were losing. She was utterly torn.

Kira and Sky stood up from their seats, grieved by what they just saw. Sky put his hand on the back of his neck and strained his head to the side, looking very uncomfortable. Kira's tiny hand rubbed Lennox's shoulder blade.

"We're going to go. We will see you at school, okay?" Kira said and walked to the door, understanding this was a private family matter. "Goodnight, Oliver," she said as she passed him to get to the front door.

Lennox nodded as she sucked in her tears. Sky gave Lennox an I-wish-I-could-do-more hug and walked out the front door with Kira. With their departure, Lennox's heart shattered all over again.

Why? That was all she wanted to know. Maybe if the *why* was answered she could finally get some sort of closure.

"Goodnight, Oliver," she said, walking past him with her chestnut brown hair in front of her face. She could not stand that he would not let her watch the news. Wasn't he just as curious as she was? The video could hold the answers.

"Goodnight. I love you," Oliver said to her as she took the first step up the stairs to her room.

"I love you too," Lennox replied, leaning over the banister to make sure he heard her. No matter how mad she was at him, she would always love him.

As she watched, tears escaped Oliver's eyes and rolled down his face. Maybe she should not have gotten so mad at him for turning off the projector. It was hard to see their parents' faces and what happened. Oliver would not want her to see him cry, but she could not leave him alone and ignore the pain that he felt. She felt it too.

All of the responsibility was on his shoulders to provide, and she had to learn to give him a break. She could not imagine what it was like to be him. They were learning day-by-awful-day that they needed each other, more now than ever.

Walking back to the living room, Lennox wrapped Oliver in a hug. He rested his head on her shoulder as his tears dripped onto her shirt. Lennox felt the warmth of the liquid seep through the cotton of her shirt and onto her skin.

"One day at a time, remember?" she whispered, hoping to be there for him like he needed her to be. Oliver picked his head off her shoulder and wiped his face with his t-shirt, darkening the already gray color.

He nodded, somehow buoyed by the familiar words. "One day at a time. I know God will get us through this."

"God?" she murmured and tilted her head.

Oh no. It came out more like a question than she had expected and knew it would cause Oliver to worry more about her. And his worry may be for a good reason. She no longer knew what she believed. She still did not understand why all of this happened, and she wanted answers. Maybe answers would settle the question of whose side God was on in this.

Oliver's eyes widened in horror. "Lennox! You can't think like that."

"I can't help it. How could God let this happen?"

Oliver gazed at Lennox intently—his every mannerism illustrated his deep concern. Lennox recognized the look. Her father gave it to her many times before. Oliver's striking resemblance to his father in looks, tone, and conviction made it impossible for Lennox to shut down the memories that began to surface. Memories of him telling Lennox all about God.

Lennox's favorite Bible story growing up was the one about the Hebrew boys who stood up for their faith and would not bow, not even under intense political pressure, not even upon threat of death. The Hebrew boys' unwavering trust in God led them to declare, "God will deliver us, and even if He doesn't, we will not bow." Something about that story always resonated deep within Lennox. The story and its message was so deeply ingrained in her heart that she could not forget, even though she almost wanted to in the midst of her pain. She wanted to trust God like they had, but the truth was, she still struggled with the "even if He doesn't" part.

Lennox averted her eyes from Oliver, afraid that he would see straight into her questioning soul. The cream living room curtains were safer so she stared at them instead. Lennox knew Oliver would not leave her alone without a reply, so she gave him the reassurance she felt she could.

"Oliver, you just have to give me some time." Lennox sighed from deep within and tried to smile. She still averted her gaze in an unsuccessful attempt to hide the tears that sprung to her eyes from thinking about her father.

Ever wise and respectful, Oliver gave his sister one last hug and then released her. His eyes narrowed again. "Lennox, you have to fight for your faith."

"Sometimes it's hard," Lennox said, staring at the ground and not wanting to get into a debate over her faith. She was already angry she struggled so much with it in the first place.

"If you don't fight for your faith, you will lose it. Your faith is worth fighting for, Lennox."

"Is it?" Her gaze locked with his. "I am not so sure anymore."

The words, touched with bitterness and anger, escaped her lips before she could stop them. Maybe she did not even want to stop them anymore.

Giving him one last, quick hug, she walked away and made her way back upstairs and closed her bedroom door behind her. She slid down the door and stared at the ceiling as thoughts coursed through her brain of what the future would be like. Her room turned in to her one place of solitude during the preceding month. The ceiling fan spun slowly and broke up her thoughts with every spin. *Why did all of this happen? Why would the Regime want my parents dead? Why hasn't God answered me? Is this how the end begins?*

All Lennox desired were answers to the new questions that were stirred up by the video and the knowledge of the terrorist cell.

Grizzly pawed the door and put her snout at the base where there was a small crack between it and the rug. Lennox stood to let the dog in, and Grizzly rammed through as soon as she opened it. She whimpered more.

"All right, get on up here." Lennox patted the open spot on her bed and Grizzly leaped to her designated area and curled up in a ball. "I thought Oliver would have needed you more tonight," Lennox commented as if she could reply. Grizzly's big, innocent brown eyes caught Lennox's as she snuggled up next to her.

Lennox prayed with a sincere heart for the first time since the silo. "Lord, I'm scared. Please let these tribulations draw me closer to you rather than push me away."

She knew that the Bible said believers would face trials of many kinds, but she wanted to know whether her trial was over, or just beginning. She wanted to know when the sun would pierce the darkness or if the world would just grow darker until darkness took over completely?

Chapter 4

Lennox was thankful Oliver let her stay home the rest of the week. Now she avoided the bombarding questions she knew her peers had about the video. She understood just as much as they did about the whole thing and she did not want to break down anymore from the haunting "I don't know." The principal and teachers were sure to understand her absence. At least, she hoped they would.

It was Saturday—prom day—and she prayed that the time and excitement of the event would distract people from asking.

Lennox heard small footsteps come up the stairs and opened the door to her bedroom. She saw Kira walk up the last steps with her arms full. She carried a shiny jewel-toned dress and makeup bag. Oliver must have let her in.

"I can't wait to do your makeup and hair! We don't have much time." She hung the dress up in Lennox's closet and set the makeup bag on the desk. Lennox knew she was overly excited. They still had four hours until prom, which was plenty of time to get ready. How much time would Kira need? If it were up to Lennox, she could be ready in less than thirty minutes.

Kira pulled a large curling iron from the bag on the desk and plugged it in. "Can you believe it is our last prom together?" Kira spun around and put Lennox's hair up in different ways to choose the best style.

"I can't," Lennox replied, unsure of whether or not she wanted to attend the prom at all. She was sure she would regret not going and would be upset to miss her final prom, but she also did not want to bring anyone else down.

"You know, if you don't want to go, I will stay with you. You are more important than any dance."

"No, I want to go. It's just hard. I really miss my parents, and I know my mom was excited to take pictures of all of us." That was all Lennox could say without tearing up, so she stopped speaking and returned to only saying a few words at a time.

"I can't imagine what you are going through. I am so sorry."

"Thanks," Lennox sucked in her breath and sat down on her bed.

Kira sat down beside her and wrapped her arm around Lennox's shoulders. Leaning in closer, Kira whispered, "I know that losing your mom and dad is something you will never get over, but it is something you have to get through. They would want you to live your life and fulfill God's purpose for your future."

Lennox knew she was right. Getting through this was her only option. Life—her life—still moved. She did not want to let it pass her by. She didn't want to live life in a walking, coma-like state. It would be okay to forget what drove her to anger for one night. She decided to focus on living.

Kira checked the curling iron and pulled the chair out from under the desk for Lennox. Lennox moved from the bed to the makeshift salon and let out a small laugh at Kira's attempts to act like a French hairstylist.

"Do whatever you want. I'm sure whatever you do will be perfect." Lennox gave a genuine smile and watched Kira in the mirror as she wrapped her hair in the hot iron. When Kira released the hair, soft, sweeping curls fell past Lennox's shoulders. After several more pieces, Kira had Lennox's hair done and swept to the side with a small jewel-encrusted hairpin. Lennox swiveled in the chair and admired Kira's handiwork.

"It's beautiful, thank you."

"You're very welcome. Now, for the makeup." Kira smiled.

Makeup was her favorite part. When they were little, she always begged Lennox to let her put makeup on her. Lennox usually surrendered and allowed it. She closed her eyes as Kira brushed on a shimmery, gold eye shadow onto her eyelids. Next came the mascara. Lennox struggled not to blink as Kira swiped her eyelashes several times with the black liquid. Kira grabbed a wide make-up brush and dabbed it into a light pink blush that she transferred to Lennox's cheeks. Polishing off Lennox's look, Kira applied a sheer red lipstick to her lips and smiled.

"All done," Kira said, swiveling the chair for Lennox to see herself better in the mirror.

"Wow, you did great! Thank you so much." Lennox was unfamiliar with seeing herself all made up, but she liked it.

She walked to the closet to grab her emerald green, satin and tulle dress—the one she so looked forward to getting. She remembered when she tried it on for the first time. She knew immediately it was the one, and her mom agreed. It was too beautiful of a dress to pass up. Her mom would have loved to see her all dolled up in it.

As Lennox got dressed, Kira finished her own makeup and hair. She gave her short hair one more spritz of hairspray. Kira turned around just as Lennox finished zipping up her dress. The ornate bodice was fitted and the skirt floated with fullness. Lennox considered it a classic Cinderella dress, except it was emerald green instead of blue. Lennox ran her hands down the full skirt, straightening out the tulle and looked up at Kira.

"Oh, Lennox, you look stunning! Absolutely beautiful."

"You think so?"

"I *know* so." Kira gave Lennox a hug. "I'm so glad you are deciding to go."

"Me too." Lennox knew they would make memories to last a lifetime.

Kira grabbed her dress from where it hung and took it off the hanger. Sliding her small frame through it, she zipped up the side. It was as beautiful as Lennox's. Small rhinestones filled its purple-hue and made Kira look like a mermaid.

"You look gorgeous." Lennox approved of Kira's dress. Its silhouette was fitted until it reached her knees and then flowed out like a mermaid's tail.

"Thank you," she said, grabbing her phone. "Let's take a picture." The two of them smiled as the camera's flash went off.

"Lennox, Sky is here!" Oliver shouted from downstairs.

"Maybe he will ask you to dance tonight," Kira posed, smiling as she opened the bedroom door to go downstairs. Lennox hoped he would but didn't count on it.

She grabbed the small jewel-encrusted clutch that rested on her bed. She could only fit her house keys and phone in it. It was not functional, but incredibly beautiful. Oliver bought it for her as a surprise for tonight. He always did something like that to cheer her up. He was a better big brother than Lennox could have asked for. He knew how difficult tonight was for her and tried to make it easier.

Kira and Lennox slowly walked downstairs to where Sky waited for both of them. He had two corsages in his hands, one for each of them. They were white roses with baby's breath tucked behind them. Sky already pinned his on the lapel of his finely pressed and perfectly fitted tuxedo. His dimples sat deeper in his cheeks tonight as his best friends came down the stairs.

"Ladies…" Sky held out his hand like a gentleman to help them both down the rest of the stairs.

Oliver took pictures and captured every detailed moment. "You guys get together and let me take a picture." Sky stood in the middle with Kira on his right and Lennox on his left. "Got it." Oliver put the camera on the table. "Let me help you with the corsages," he added as he grabbed one to put on Lennox.

Kira smiled at Lennox because of the fatherly role Oliver demonstrated.

After a few more pictures, they said goodbye to Oliver and piled into Sky's single-cab truck. It was old and rugged. Its ancient, navy-blue paint chipped away. Sky's dad promised to restore it and polish it up once he returned from deployment, but that had not happened yet. His dad was still deployed. Sky had no idea where. That was sensitive information that his dad was not allowed to share. Lennox hoped that maybe Sky's dad could answer questions she had about the Regime when he returned from duty. He had to know something she didn't.

Although Kira was smaller, she insisted that Lennox sit in the middle closest to Sky. Lennox was glad that it was dark enough outside to hide her rosy cheeks as she sat close to him all dressed up. The truck rolled into a parking space in front of a grand hotel. The student council reserved it long in advance for the prom. This hotel was the envy of all schools for a prom location. There was no better place in town—or eighty miles, for that matter.

A path through a garden of red roses led them to the large ballroom where their fellow classmates already began the festivities. Lennox inhaled deeply and took in the light, pleasant scent of the sweet roses. It reminded her so much of the perfume her mother used to wear. The prom's theme, *A Happily Ever After*, floated in lights on the stone building as a cascading waterfall fell into a fountain to the right of them. Lennox closed her eyes and opened them slowly. She could do this, for one night she could enjoy herself.

Chapter 5

Lennox walked into what she knew was a night to remember. The ballroom housed a magnificent crystal chandelier that hung in the center of the room and radiated iridescent light onto the dance floor. She watched her beautiful peers in ball gowns and tuxedos grace the dance floor with their presence. It was as if they were back in time to when society was more elegant. Elaborate and expensive tiles that glistened from the light the chandelier provided surrounded the hardwood dance floor. Round tables draped with golden cloth were available for those who preferred to sit. Chaperones stood to the side and mingled.

Lennox forgot her troubles for a little while and let good emotions run through her. Her eyes roamed the extravagant décor as she secretly wished Sky would ask her for a slow dance. She followed Sky and made her way to one of the tables. A slow song filled the air with its melody. Kira nudged Lennox and caused her to bump Sky's back ever so slightly.

"Lennox, would you like to dance?" Sky turned around and held out his hand. It was almost as if he and Kira secretly planned this moment.

"I would love to." Lennox turned back to Kira as if to say "Thank you." Kira nodded and motioned for her to go on to the dance floor and have fun.

Sky led Lennox by the hand past an ice sculpture of a castle and out onto the dance floor. He placed his hands on her waist. She rested her arms high on his shoulders and followed his lead. They swayed side-to-side in the center of the room underneath the brilliance of the chandelier. Its light glistened on Lennox's dress like the stars in the night. The emerald green fabric flattered the gold flecks in her hazel eyes. The tulle of her dress flowed with her movement as she danced with Sky, who was surprisingly a very good dancer. She never guessed he was because he only danced to the upbeat music that played at former proms. In this tiny moment, life was perfect—if only for a little while. The song that played was soft piano with minimal lyrics.

Sky tucked a loose curl behind Lennox's ear and pressed his forehead to hers. "You know I am here for you, no matter what." His eyes and heart were fixed on Lennox.

"I know, and I am forever grateful for that." She could not utter her true feelings just yet.

She rested her head against his chest and stayed there until the last note of the song played. When the song transitioned to something a little faster, they lingered for a moment, then released their embrace and walked back to where Kira waited for them. She was talking to a boy who had a crush on her since Lennox could remember, but Kira was focused more on having a relationship with God than she was with having a relationship with any boy.

Kira had her fair share of boy drama sophomore year and made a vow to get her life right with God before getting involved with boys who made her heart stray from her first love, Jesus Christ. Lennox admired Kira for her unashamed faith in Christ and always thought she could learn a thing or two from her. Her parents loved it when Kira came over because they knew how good of an influence she was on Lennox.

Before Sky and Lennox reached Kira, the ambience was rocked into oblivion by an ear-shattering bang. The walls of the building heaved and pitched from the reverberation. Lennox was frozen flat on her back as she gasped for air while dust particles rained down from the roof. Embers floated around her like fireflies in the spring-time. Everything moved in slow motion. She heard nothing except the squealing in her ears. It sounded like fingernails running across a chalkboard. Her sight was blurry and her head pounded. The once beautiful chandelier no longer held its place on the ceiling, but was now shattered into a thousand shards of irreparable glass. Exposed wires threatened to set the ballroom ablaze with every orange spark.

What's happening?

Lennox squinted to see through the falling ashes. Knots twisted in her stomach and made her want to throw up. When she rolled her head to the right, she saw a boy's body slumped on the wooden floor.

Sky? Oh God, please, no.

One minute Lennox saw beams of light, the next she saw black. Smoke rose to the ceiling and fires whipped through the building. The sweltering heat made Lennox sick. Hot liquid covered her skin. She touched her hand to her chest. The warmth of her own blood filled her palm. She was in too much shock to feel any pain. She only felt a throbbing sensation near her heart. She tried to stand up, but she could not move. Her body was paralyzed.

I am going to die.

Dizziness overtook her and the walls around her spun wildly out of control. Her senses came and went as she drifted in and out of consciousness. The next thing Lennox remembered was a voice yelling close to her side, "You have to help her! She is bleeding out!" Then she heard another voice yell from a distance. "I got her. I got her!"

Lennox felt someone strong lift her up and run. The jarring up and down made her nauseous.

"Hang in there Lennox," Sky's voice pleaded. "Stay with me."

All Lennox thought was how glad she was that Sky was okay. The loss of blood made Lennox light headed again. She heard unfamiliar voices yelling back and forth. Blue and red lights swirled through her eyelids and sirens filled her eardrums.

"We have a female, seventeen-years-old, with shrapnel wounds near her heart, it barely missed her artery," the unfamiliar voice said.

Lying flat on a bed with wheels that swiveled around, every bump on the hospital floors made Lennox panic.

Now time moved too fast. The sheet that covered her felt heavy on her chest. They wheeled her through huge double doors to an operating room and placed a mask over her face. The tubes to her mask made an airy sound. She breathed it in. Heaviness seeped into her veins and then into her muscles and bones until she felt no part of herself. The surgical lights were too bright. A man leaned over her, casting a shadow onto her face as he blocked out the harsh light.

"You're going to be all right," he said as she fought to hang onto consciousness. "Take deep breaths."

Lennox inhaled and exhaled deeper with wide and uncertain eyes. The doctor's kind face slipped away from her sight. For one split second, fear radiated through her body, and then it gave way to nothing.

Chapter 6

Bright light consumed Lennox's vision. She thought it was the same surgical light she saw before and wondered if she was awake from the operation already.

But she wasn't in the operating room.

When her eyes finally focused, there was a surreal beauty all around her. A sense of peace encompassed her. She was dressed in a white dress that flowed with the breeze. She looked down at her chest and her wound was gone. Not even a scar. Nothing was broken and nothing was missing. Colors were vivid again—perhaps more vivid—and there were some she had never seen before. Yellows, blues, oranges, and greens mixed to form new brilliant shades that were impossibly beautiful.

This was not a realm of earth. At least, she did not think it was. Lennox knew she was dreaming. It had to be. A beautiful dream with trees and flowers that were different somehow. Their shapes exceeded what the natural earth could do. Lennox took a step forward to a patch of flowers, mesmerized by the inherent beauty of every petal. They shimmered as if dipped in glitter.

She felt weightless, as if she walked on air. Gravity had no hold of her. Reaching down, she picked a flower from the dirt and put it up to her nose. Before she took the breath, another one immediately grew in its place. A ravishing scent rushed across her sense of smell. It was so intoxicating she almost tasted it. It was a fragrance so pure and clean, it was like nothing she ever smelled before.

Lennox turned in every direction, and all she found was breathtaking scenery.

A choir of angel voices lifted in praise overtook the sound in her ears. It grew in her spirit, making her feel whole and complete. A peaceful sense of comfort rushed over her as if she knew she lacked nothing in this place. Lennox closed her eyes and lifted her head with her arms outstretched and took it all in. She let the calm drown her in peace. With her eyes closed, every other sense multiplied.

Birds sang, trees whistled, and flowers tickled across her ankles in a dance. The wind swept through her hair and gave her goosebumps. It rushed new life into her. There was no pain, no fear, no questions. Only utter and complete tranquility. The chorus of angels turned into a symphony of stringed instruments.

Her feet itched to dance to the soul-inspiring music, so she did. In one breath of experiencing it, she found her passion in this place. She turned with grace and ease. Her arms were weightless as feathers floating in the air. Her steps matched the rhythm of the strings. She had never danced like this at school. There she was still a beginner, but in this place her dance was effortless. She forgot about her cares and her troubles as if they never even existed. She was more alive than ever, and that was all she knew. She was more herself than ever before.

She opened her eyes to what she knew was unreal, but was startled to find her parents standing not more than thirty feet in front of her. Her mother's auburn hair glistened and her face glowed with radiance. Her father's face was unwrinkled and clean-shaven. An unfathomable light shined from within him. Joy filled her as she hastened to greet them, but she was there with just the thought of going to them. Somehow, she transported herself from one point to the next with only the thought of going.

"Mom? Dad?" She reached out to touch them.

Without hesitation, they stretched out their arms and embraced her in a hug. The power of their love wrapped around her. This was not a dream. It was something else, but she could not figure out what. She rested her head on her mother's shoulder. Her perfume was as sweet as the flower Lennox picked earlier. Both of their heads rested on top of Lennox's. Their cheeks pressed into her hair. She squeezed them back, not willing to relinquish them from her grasp. Never again did she want to let go of their embrace.

Then, like a rush, her questions returned, but not in the way she thought they would. She was still at peace, even though the questions remained. She was about to ask them when they both simultaneously whispered into her ear the very same word. Their voices joined in unison like the brush of an angel's wing.

"Fight."

Their arms vanished from around her. They returned to the air from where they came. They were gone. Lennox turned in circles, trying to find them again.

"Mom, come back. Dad, where are you?"

When she could not find them, she returned to the word they spoke. The one word that meant so much but told her so little.

Fight? For what? Fight for my faith? Fight for them?

Lennox focused again on her efforts to find them. She had to find them. With the thought, she transported herself to every angle that she could, but they were nowhere to be found. There was not even a trace of them.

In the distance, Lennox comprehended a kingdom appearing, and it was grander and far more splendid than any kingdom of earth. There were streets of gold and walls of jasper. Gates of pearl were around the entire circumference of the kingdom spanned out before her. She was mesmerized by it so much that she forgot her search. At that moment, something in her told her she found where her parents were.

The sound of water flowed. A light—brighter than the one before—blinded her eyes.

She took a deep breath. She knew this place. Her dad told her in detail about it on the silo roof. She knew what the kingdom was. It was Heaven.

Am I dead?

She heard the hospital machines beeping in the background. Doctors spoke, but she could not make out their words. Their voices talked over one another. The mask was removed from her face. The medicine wore off.

"Lennox, can you open your eyes for me?"

The same doctor with the gentle face leaned over her again. What was his name? She could hear the nurses call him Dr. Car… Carls… Carlson. That was it. His name was Dr. Carlson. Her eyelids felt like bricks over her eyes. She willed herself to open them, but only one listened.

"That's okay, sweetheart, your surgery went well. We are taking you to recovery now," he said.

The pain medicine knocked her out again, but this time, there were no visions of Heaven.

Chapter 7

"She is one lucky girl." Lennox overheard the doctor talk to someone in the hall and knew he spoke about her." She died on the table but we were able to revive her quickly. One more inch to the left and she would have been dead—no matter what we did to try to save her."

She could not force her eyelids open yet. They were sealed shut, begging the rest of her body to sleep. She obeyed them for a little while longer. She drifted back into unconsciousness.

Eight hours later, the morning sunrise pierced through her hospital room window and filled the air with tiny dust particles. Her eyelids fluttered awake. The white walls reflected the light.

The first person she saw was Sky. He sat on a chair

next to her bed with his head rested on the bed's railing. His black hair was covered with ash and his face covered in soot. His clothes smelled of fire and his shirt looked bloody.

With her blood.

Tired eyes shot up to meet hers. "She's awake," Sky said to Oliver, who slept on the other side of the bed.

Oliver grabbed her hand and squeezed it tight. He stood to his feet and leaned over the rail to give her a kiss on the forehead. "You gave us a pretty good scare there for a while," Oliver said with his eyes soft and caring.

"The doctor's said you are lucky to be alive," Sky added.

Lennox gave both of them a slight smile. She heard what the doctor said. It was a miracle she was alive. She wanted to tell them what she saw when her body slipped into death, and she wanted to tell Oliver what their mom and dad said, but her voice was not ready to speak. Her eyelids turned to bricks, too heavy to keep open.

Oliver brushed her hair back with his hand. "Go back to sleep, it's okay."

Lennox's body would recover faster if she slept. Her mind fought, but her body won the battle. She slept.

Lennox hoped to revisit that beautiful place, but instead, her dreams turned to nightmares and sleep was torture. Her injured classmates were plastered on the walls of her mind. Their blood was all she saw. *How many more were injured? How many more were like the boy on the floor? What about Kira? Where was she now?* Her heart raced with uncertainty. She had to find out what happened to everyone.

She shook herself awake. Sweat dripped from her face and nerves chattered inside of her.

Sky was right where she left him. He felt her body shake and tried to calm her.

"Shhh... you're okay. You're safe," he whispered.

Lennox's voice pushed through her lips. She had to find out. "Kira?"

Sky looked at her and hesitated for a minute. "She is in the ICU and has not woken up yet."

Lennox's spirit was crushed. She rolled her head to the other side of her pillow. It was cold on her cheek. Oliver sat down, leaning his head against the windowpane. His breath left a circle of fog on the glass.

"Oliver?" she mumbled. Her voice scratched through her windpipes.

Oliver raised his head from the window and the fog

disappeared from the glass. He walked over, taking her hand as he sat beside her. "What is it?"

"I just want you close." Tears pricked her eyes once again.

The nurses' station projector pixelated images in the hall. The holograms of the hotel bombing filled the hospital hallway. Reporters' voices occupied the airwaves.

"We have just learned that the terrorist cell called 'the Regime' is responsible for the recent attacks at a hotel which was hosting a local school prom. A dozen students have died from the blasts that were set off at the Renais Hotel. Hundreds more are wounded and in critical condition. Our thoughts and prayers go out to the families of the victims."

Sky jumped up and shut the door behind him. "You know you should be a little more sensitive to what your patients have been through!" Sky yelled so loud that Lennox could hear him through the closed door.

None of them wanted a replay of what they endured, but Lennox could not help but hear the name "Regime" and wonder about it. Everything changed in her world so rapidly. One moment she was a happy teenage dreamer with lofty goals, and the next she almost dies by the hand of the same terrorist group that murdered her parents. What was the world coming to? Why hadn't the government stopped them yet?

The image of the emblem with the snake coiling around a staff infiltrated her mind. The urge to share what she saw while her body faded overtook Lennox, so she blurted out, "I saw Mom and Dad." She knew their message was not only for her, but for Oliver as well. It had to be.

Oliver looked concerned. "Lennox, I see Mom and Dad in my dreams too. It's normal. It's okay."

Lennox's vision was anything but normal. She hoped Oliver believed her. She barely believed it herself. She mustered the courage to speak about it. "No, this time, it was different. I saw them, and it was so real I did not want to let go of them. I think God gave me this dream for a reason. Mom and Dad whispered one word and then vanished."

"What did they say?" Oliver asked, intrigued. Lennox noticed how his curiosity rose at her mention of God's involvement in her life.

"They said, 'fight.' That was it. That was all they said." She grabbed both of Oliver's hands and flinched from pain. "I know we have to fight for our faith. I'm just scared that something bad will happen… bad is all that seems to happen now."

Oliver stood straight and squared his shoulders. "That is why we have to fight… so that we can change the bad."

She hoped he was right. She hoped it was possible to change the bad around them.

Chapter 8

Fight took residence in Lennox. Her feet hit the cold white tile of the hospital floor, the monotony of the flooring broken with specks of blue. Sky finally went home to rest and Oliver left to pull the truck around to patient pick-up. Lennox—still weak—wobbled back and forth every time she stood. Staring at one blue speck until the spinning stopped helped keep her head straight.

The nurse came with a wheelchair.

"I don't need a wheelchair, I'm okay." Lennox looked up at her.

The nurse watched Lennox struggle to stand as she pleaded her case, but she knew the drill and shook her head "No."

"Sorry child… hospital rules." She lowered Lennox into the chair.

She was a robust nurse with a big personality and was one of Lennox's favorites during her stay at the hospital.

Lennox wondered if her mother knew her, but suspected she didn't since the nurse never mentioned anything. Her mother worked as a triage nurse at this hospital for years until she moved to a doctor's office not too long ago.

The nurse placed gentle hands on Lennox's shoulders and gave them a light squeeze. Lennox knew she would let her walk if the rules allowed it and if she were not so shaky. The wheelchair rolled out of Lennox's room and down the hall past the nurse's station.

"Can you take me by Kira Heston's room before I leave?" Lennox asked before she turned the corner to the elevator.

"I'm not supposed to, but I will just this once, understand?"

"Yes, ma'am, thank you." Lennox nodded her head.

The nurse pushed her farther down the hall to room 304. The wheelchair stopped outside of Kira's door and Lennox watched helplessly as the machines made Kira's chest rise and fall. The beeps set a steady rhythm. Lennox matched her breathing to it.

Kira's purple dress was gone and a hospital gown took its place. Tubes covered Kira's face. Lennox barely saw any part of her friend's features, but what was visible looked swollen and bruised. It was hard for

Lennox to see her beautiful friend so defenseless. Her short, dark hair—previously hair-sprayed to perfection—was now brushed to the side by the hands of her loving parents. They sat on both sides of her hospital bed, asleep as their hands held hers. Their gray hair made them look like Kira's grandparents. They had Kira late in life and claimed she was their miracle child.

Lennox felt lucky to have her as a friend. She helped her keep her head on straight. She could not imagine her world without Kira in it. Kira *had* to survive. She had so much living left to do. Lennox remembered the dreams they shared about their futures. They were going to college together. They wanted to travel the world together.

She lowered her head and let the tears gather in her eyelashes. Lennox wished she could switch places with Kira and take the pain away, but she couldn't. She hated it.

Kira's monitors lost their steady beat and emitted irregular chimes that stretched out for long periods of time. Kira's mom and dad lifted their heads. They looked at the alarms and then at each other. The beeping grew louder, and soon nurses rushed past Lennox and into Kira's room. Kira's parents stood to their feet as nurses gently pushed them out of the way.

Frantic, Lennox rose from the wheelchair as her vision was impeded. "What's happening?"

Lennox's nurse lowered her back into the chair as Kira's door slammed closed and completely shut Lennox out. Lennox stared at her nurse, waiting for some sort of explanation that everything would be okay and that the monitors and rush of nurses was merely a precaution. But deep down she knew something was wrong… terribly wrong.

"Lennox, your brother is waiting for you. I should get you to him," the nurse said.

"Please, I can't leave until I know she is okay. She's my best friend," Lennox said, looking at the closed door. She vaguely heard what took place on the other side.

"I'll go tell your brother. Please, at least stay in the chair."

The nurse walked down the hall and turned the corner to the elevator, giving Lennox one sorrowful glance and leaving her in place.

Lennox waited in the chair outside of Kira's room for five minutes… ten minutes. The crisp, white walls of the hospital hall made Lennox feel even lonelier. Oliver came from around the corner and rushed to Lennox's side. Lennox saw him and started to break down.

"What is it?"

"It's Kira. Her monitors went off. No one will tell me anything."

Oliver crouched beside the wheelchair and bowed his head as he waited with Lennox. Restless and tired of waiting, Oliver stood up and stretched, and then crouched back down next to Lennox's side. Another twenty minutes passed before the door opened and the nurses walked out with their heads low, avoiding eye contact with Lennox as they walked by her. No eye contact was necessary. Not even words were necessary. Lennox knew immediately that her friend was gone.

She watched as Kira's mom and dad leaned their heads on her forehead and gave her lifeless body a kiss. As they both cried, they looked at the door where Lennox so patiently waited. Their eyes fell back down to look at Kira and then back up at Lennox. Kira's dad shook his head for a brief second and walked to the door to give Lennox permission to say goodbye. Goodbye to one of her truest and most precious of friends—one of her pillars of strength was gone.

Life felt like it was being sucked out of Lennox. She hyperventilated when the truth of losing Kira sunk in, slow and steady. Her heart dropped so low and fast she was not sure she could ever bring it back from the depths. Why did she live and Kira die? Lennox's heart wanted to harden again, but the vision of Heaven would not let it.

Fight.

She would not let her heart grow callused. She knew Kira was in God's hands and that she was in that beautiful place—a place she would stay if she had the choice.

Oliver rolled Lennox's chair by Kira's side. No one spoke while Lennox held Kira's cooling hand and rested her head on top of it. Her world was devastated all over again. Lennox wanted to stay there and hold Kira's hand forever. She knew this was the last time she could hold it. Though she'd been taught a person's body was only the shell, it did not make it any easier for Lennox to let go.

She knew she eventually had to.

Chapter 9

It was too soon for Lennox to attend another funeral for someone she loved. Yet, here she was again, slipping on the same black dress she wore to her parents'. She would be eternally grateful if she never had to wear this dress again. Death should not be such a normal part of a seventeen-year-old's life. Not this many. Not this close.

Oliver helped Lennox into the truck. Her body molded to the front seat as he drove down the serene road lined by perfect houses in perfect rows—a contrast to life's imperfections. The dark cloud that loomed over Lennox's world overshadowed the tranquility of the bright and sunny day. Her heart hurt and her mind still tried to make her doubt. Why wouldn't she doubt after all she had been through? After all she had lost?

When they arrived at the church, dozens of families dressed in black were represented. Too many buried their loved ones because of the Regime. The Regime stole so much from Lennox, she already developed an intense hate for them. If she ever got the chance, she would stop them. But she had no idea how anything she did could make a difference. She was one girl, and they were a demented army.

Lilacs—Kira's favorite flower—lined the altar as she entered the sanctuary. Their aroma permeated the room. A picture of Kira was placed on a gold easel. It was her senior picture, taken before she cut off all of her hair. Her soft curls were tucked behind her ears and her smile ran all the way up her rosy cheeks to her brown eyes.

As Oliver and Lennox walked down the church aisle, Lennox saw Sky already in his seat behind Kira's family. She walked through the pews, took her seat, and gave Sky a warm embrace. His eyes were red from crying—though tears no longer fell.

When the funeral began, Oliver grabbed Lennox's hand and held it like her father would have. Sky held the other and gripped it tight during the beautiful speeches from family members. Kira touched so many people's lives. She was a light in a dark world that was snuffed out too soon. The attack on that fateful day changed them all forever.

The tormented cries of Kira's family pierced right

through Lennox. She knew the pain they felt. She knew what the loss of a loved one meant. It meant hundreds— if not thousands—of questions that would never be answered. Her soul hurt for them as she mourned with them.

The preacher spoke words of peace to the hurting congregation. His words captured Lennox's attention. She listened as he spoke.

"Sometimes we go through things in life and we don't understand why. But the important thing is that we understand God has not forsaken us. He will bring peace to the hurting. We do not mourn as the world mourns. We know there is hope after death."

Hope—a concept Lennox wanted so desperately to believe in.

A still, small voice whispered through the pain in Lennox's heart. *I am right here with you. I have never left your side.* Goosebumps rose on her arms. Lennox gasped and bowed her head. Her heart pounded in her chest from the powerful whisper that spoke louder than anything else. It was the answer to the question she asked on top of the silo. God knew the questions she had in her heart and saw all she lost. The faith that was born in her soul when she was younger started to reignite. It became stronger and more tangible. Confidence filled her. Something better waited on the other side of the struggle. She saw it. God showed it to her. Only hope in eternal life eased her pain. It was worth fighting for. *Faith* was worth fighting for. She began to understand that now.

At that moment, she prayed from the depths of her soul with eyes shut tight. "Lord, forgive me for doubting you. Jesus, I need you. I can't do this anymore without you."

Lennox hoped she could hold on to the resurgence of faith once she went back to the reality of her life. The reality that a terrorist group called the Regime stole everything good away from her. They took her family, her friend, her safety, and made her question her God. Never again would she give them that much power.

Never again.

Chapter 10

Two days after Kira's funeral, Lennox found herself not wanting to do much of anything. Her heart still mended from both physical and spiritual wounds. Events unfolding in her life left her with more than just the scar on her chest. There were invisible scars deeper than any flesh wound that only she and God saw. She did not want to become like a fearful hermit crab tucked away in its shell, but she was exactly that, hiding in her room. Neither Oliver nor Sky were permitted entry.

Her solitude did not help. She craved human interaction, so she decided to sit quietly downstairs. With her blanket wrapped tightly around her like a cocoon, she rested her head on the arm of the sofa in the living room. Oliver sat down beside her and cleared his throat. His eyes grew serious and his posture stretched taller.

"Lennox, we need to talk."

Lennox felt chilled at the sight of his serious face and devoted herself to listen to whatever he was going to say. She unburied herself from the blanket and sat up, looking at him as if he was far off. His serious tone concerned her and she trembled at the thought of more bad news. "What is it?" she asked, scrunching her eyebrows together, needing to know.

"You're not going to like this, but I feel like it is something I need to do… I am supposed to do."

"Just tell me, please." She wanted to hear whatever he was going to say, and fast.

"I am going to join the military." His hazel eyes shifted back and forth looking into hers.

"The military? But… you can't!" It was like a swift punch to her gut that knocked the breath out of her. She did not want to lose Oliver too. He was the only family she had left. Then she remembered her vision. Maybe this is what her parents meant when they spoke to her.

Fight, fight, fight… the word grew clear and attached itself to meaning.

"Lennox, the Regime killed Mom and Dad, Kira, and they almost killed you. I have to do something. I cannot sit back and pretend like I am okay anymore. There have been too many attacks against the people I love. I have to fight."

He was right. There were too many attacks against them personally. She wanted something done about it, but not at the expense of losing him.

"I don't want to lose you."

"You won't. God will watch over me."

The vision echoed again and again in her mind.

Fight.

She had to fight for her faith just as Oliver felt he had to fight in the erupting war. It was another test of faith that Lennox would endure.

"How long before you leave?" Lennox asked barely above a whisper.

"Not long, they need recruits as soon as possible. I only have a couple of days. I made arrangements for you to be able to stay with Sky and his grandpa."

Lennox had not even thought about where she would live with Oliver gone. She could not imagine staying home alone. It would not be home without him.

Grizzly stood by Lennox's side as she prepared her heart for Oliver's departure. The affectionate canine bumped into Lennox so she would pet her. Sometimes Lennox wished she could be as oblivious to the world as Grizzly was.

Lennox made breakfast for Oliver as she waited for him to come downstairs. His bags clipped the banister one spindle at a time as he raced down the steps.

"I am going to miss you," Lennox said when he arrived in the kitchen, trying to hide any fear she had of losing him. She focused on spreading the cream cheese on his bagel.

"I am going to miss you too. I will send hologram messages to you every week, and I will be back before you know it." Oliver raised Lennox's head up and gave her a gentle hug, making sure he did not hurt her healing wound.

"Here, I know you probably won't get any of these while you are at training." She handed him the bagel. It was a pitiful farewell gift, but it was all she could think of. He was not allowed to take a lot of material possessions with him.

"Thanks." He let out a small laugh.

She knew he would miss the little things—like bagels and cream cheese. She shook her head. Oliver walked to the living room as he took bites of his bagel and threw his bags on the couch. Lennox followed close behind and looked past the cream colored curtains of the living room window.

An armored Humvee pulled in front of the house. It looked out of place in her neighborhood, but with a war that threatened the nation, the military did whatever they could to help get more boots on the ground.

Oliver opened the front door. "I will be right out!" he shouted to the men. He faced Lennox. "Sky is on his way to take you to his house." His words seemed prophetic as Sky's old truck turned into the driveway. Oliver gave her a huge hug and kiss on the forehead, "I love you, kiddo."

"I love you too." She hugged him back too tight. She did not want to let go. She did not know when, or if, she would see him again. Oliver cupped her cheeks with both hands and pressed his forehead against hers.

"Everything is going to work out. You're going to be okay," he said.

"I hope so," she replied.

"I have something for you. Mom's will said to give this to you on your eighteenth birthday, but since I will be at training, I want you to have it now. She said it was important."

A necklace dangled from Oliver's finger. It was her

mother's locket. The heart-shaped necklace—designed with the image of a sparrow inlayed in gold—swung back and forth. It was the very locket her mother wore every single day. Dad gave it to her mother as a gift in the hospital on the day Lennox was born. Lennox opened it. On the left was a picture of Oliver when he was three-years-old, and on the right was her newborn picture. She turned the locket over. Their mother's favorite verse was engraved into the gold, "We walk by faith, not by sight."

Lennox's mom lived by that verse. She did not see things as they were, but rather through eyes of faith. Any bad news received was met by her quoting that exact scripture. Lennox's heart swelled inside her chest with love. Instead of tears, the locket brought a smile. Her parents were in God's hands just as Kira was. The locket was now her daily reminder. She no longer looked at everything she went through with physical sight. She looked at it through faith, like her mother did. Life was too short to live without hope.

"Thank you so much for giving it to me early." She was glad not to wait until eighteen to have it. "I will wear it every day."

Lennox clasped the necklace around her neck. Her fingers held on to the locket, sliding it along the chain.

The shiny metal was cool to the touch but warmed the longer she held on to it. Oliver kissed the top of her head and then called for Grizzly.

"Come on, Grizz. You are going with me." Oliver opened the front door and headed down the sidewalk with Grizzly by his side and Lennox behind him.

Grizzly was the smartest dog Lennox ever saw. The retired police dog never lost her training. Oliver got clearance for her to join the K9 unit because he knew she would help in the fight. Lennox cuddled her one last time and buried her face in Grizzly's fur. Grizzly nuzzled Lennox back.

"I am going to miss you, Grizz. Take care of Oliver for me." Lennox kissed her between her big, brown eyes.

When Lennox let her go, she ran to Oliver's side in obedience. Sky got out of his truck and stood on the sidewalk by Oliver. Oliver clasped Sky's hand and brought him close to pat him on the back.

"Watch out for Lennox, okay?"

"Don't worry, I will." Sky was full of confidence.

Oliver let Grizzly in the rear of the vehicle first. Her back legs lunged as she jumped in with ease. Her tongue dripped with drool as her face hung out of the window. Oliver hopped in next to her. The driver did not wait any longer. He put the Humvee in gear and drove away. Oliver signed *I love you* to Lennox as the vehicle accelerated. Lennox watched him all the way down their cookie-cutter street with the perfect rows of houses until she could not see him anymore. Her heart mourned as if she had lost him forever.

Her brother was gone.

Lord, please don't let me lose him too.

Sky held Lennox in his arms to comfort her as her head rested on his chest. His cotton t-shirt was stained with her tears. She had to leave this place. The house behind her was no longer home.

She pulled herself away from Sky and went in the barren house to gather what few belongings she decided were worth taking with her. Material possessions mattered less to her now. All she needed were a few clothes, her journal, and her Bible—she committed herself to reading it more.

Chapter 11

With a photo of her family held tightly to her chest, Lennox sat in the front seat of Sky's truck as it traveled down the old dirt road that led to his house in the country. She determined to keep her family close in spirit, even if they were absent in flesh. She kept her mother and father's legacy alive. Precious memories of them sustained her and made her push through the hardness of life.

The old truck kicked up dirt, leaving a trail of dust in its wake. Sky's house was the picture of country perfection. Its wooden planks were painted light yellow while the wrap-around porch was painted white. A renovated bright red door sat off to the left side. For as old as the house was it still looked brand new, like it was just built.

Hopping out of the truck, Sky walked around to the passenger's side to help Lennox out. He opened the door for her. The soles of her leather boots touched the dusty road. She squeezed the picture in her hands tighter.

"Here, let me carry your bag." Sky took the bag off her shoulder and carried it for her.

"Grandpa! Lennox is here!" Sky yelled as they walked through the door.

Sky's mom abandoned him when he was just a baby. She said that she could not handle being a military wife—left all alone to raise a child. So she left Sky with his grandpa when he was one-year-old. He had not heard from her since. At least his grandpa was kind and loving. He never left Sky.

Sky's grandpa appeared from the back of the house. Despite being confined to a wheelchair, he moved swiftly and turned expertly around every angle.

"Hi, Lennox," he said as he pulled Lennox down and wrapped his arms around her. His bald head smelled of aftershave and peppermint.

Lennox always wondered what he looked like when he was younger because of how handsome he was, even without hair. His piercing eyes were the purest blue and reminded her of an ocean painting she once saw. His wrinkled and sun-spotted skin contributed to his warmth, rather than his age. He was young in spirit and very much alive and exuberant.

"Hi, Mr. Conners. Thank you for letting me stay here with you guys. It means a lot," Lennox said as she stood up straight. She owed this man a great debt for taking her in when she had nowhere else to go.

"It is our pleasure to have you stay with us. I made up the guest room for you, and it has its own bathroom so you don't have to share with Sky," he said with a smirk. "Sky, why don't you show Lennox her room." He motioned to a room down the hall.

Sky escorted Lennox down the narrow walkway. Pictures of his family lined the walls in an old fashioned way. His school year photos were too adorable for Lennox to avoid.

"You were so cute." She let the words out before she could stop them. Her cheeks grew hot. She was sure her face was red.

"I *was* pretty cute, wasn't I?" he joked.

Sky tried to stay lighthearted, but in the wake of Kira's funeral he grew more somber than usual. Lennox was glad to see his face light up with a smile, but she was also thankful he did not guide the conversation to her opinion on his present appearance. Her feelings seemed petty after the seriousness of their shared tragedies.

Lennox noticed another picture—it was Sky's parents. His dad wore the dress blues of the Army, and his mother had on a formal dress that showed her pregnant belly. She rested her hand on top of the bump and appeared happy about her pregnancy—at least, she did in the picture. His mother did not look like the type to leave her family behind. But then, what did an abandoning mother look like anyway?

Sky noticed her admiring his parents' picture. "That was taken at the Capital Ball before my dad was deployed. Right before I was born." Sky's pain was evident.

It appeared his mother left an invisible scar on his heart. Lennox could tell it still hurt that his mom left him and that his dad was absent. His dad returned after a few years of deployment, only to be deployed again.

"Have you heard from him at all?" she asked.

"Not since about a year ago. He had to stop all contact for a special op he was leading. I don't even know where he is." He turned back around.

"It must be hard not knowing where someone you love is," Lennox pondered inwardly. She felt the same about Oliver's departure. She did not like the fact that she would not know where he was or what he would face.

Sky pointed to an open doorway. "Here it is. Just let my grandpa know if you need anything. He loves to help."

"It's nice, thank you."

Sky was careful not to step foot in the room. Lennox looked at him strangely, unsure of why he would not cross a very clear line between her borrowed room and the hall.

"My grandpa said to be respectful and never go into your room." He laughed as he walked away. She knew he was serious. His grandpa was nice, but strict and very old fashioned.

The room smelled of fresh linens. The bedding was crisp and in perfect order. There was an antique desk and chair nestled under a window. Lennox thought it might be a nice place to write and pray. She took in all of her new surroundings. Maybe her spirit could heal better here. This was her new safe haven. This was her new home.

Home... a place she badly needed.

Lennox put pen to paper as she sat at the antique desk. It was the first time she wrote in days. It was nice to let out all of the emotions bottled up inside. Everything that built up found its way onto the page and she sighed as the heaviness lifted. She set her pen down and opened the white plantation shutters before her. She daydreamed as she stared out the window... daydreamed about better days.

Rain trickled from the clouds. It left a light mist on the windowsill. Deer roamed the fields and grazed on the grass without a care in the world. There was not another house to be seen. It was cozy being away from all of the noise. A gentle knock on Lennox's door broke her trance. She turned around in her chair. It was Mr. Conners.

"I don't mean to bother you, but lunch will be ready in a little bit if you want some."

The air from the kitchen wafted into Lennox's room. He made pot roast and rolls for lunch. Lennox hoped he had not gone out of his way on her behalf.

"I will be right there. It smells delicious," she smiled.

Lennox walked into the kitchen. The floral wallpaper on the walls was old, but pristine. The counters were filled with antiques and the table set with cream-colored dishes and ornate silverware. Homemade buttered rolls sat in a basket covered with a light blue napkin to maintain their warmth. The roast was set on a nice serving dish.

Sky saw the look of worry on Lennox's face. He knew she felt bad that his grandpa went through all of this trouble.

"Don't worry. He does this every weekend," Sky grinned. He looked up at his happy grandfather who rolled up to the table, ready to eat.

Lennox breathed a sigh of relief. Mr. Conners went through a lot of unnecessary trouble if he intended to impress her. She was already impressed he volunteered to take her in and was glad to discover Mr. Conners did not go out of his way on her account. He already did more than enough.

Mr. Conners prayed over their meal and served their plates immediately after they said *amen.*

"Have either of you heard about how Kira's parents are doing?" Mr. Conners darted his eyes between Lennox and Sky. He knew Kira quite well from the years he babysat them all together when they were little.

"I called them the other day. They are doing as well as can be expected," Lennox answered, wiping her mouth with a napkin.

It was hard to speak to them. Lennox never really knew what to say, but she wanted to let them know she was there for them as they were for her. Lennox refused to let Kira's memory be forgotten, and she wanted Kira's parents to know that.

"I've been praying for them," he said. Lennox knew that was true. She heard him pray before—very powerful prayers.

"Me too," Sky added as he cleared his throat. A tinge of pain returned to his face. However strong he tried to appear around others, Lennox knew he hurt as much as she did.

They lowered their heads and finished eating. Memories of the bombing were sobering and hurt to the core. It made them acknowledge the harsh truth of their mortality. Life was but a fleeting moment—a leaf in the wind. Here one moment and gone the next.

Sky's fork scraped against the cream plate as he scooped seconds. Lennox gathered her dishes and started to grab the rest, but Mr. Conners shook his head as he raised the napkin to his face and wiped the corners of his mouth.

"I will get them," he said, motioning for Lennox to sit back down.

"Please, let me clear the table." Lennox reached for Mr. Conners' plate. Her mom taught her to be a polite houseguest ever since she was young. She felt it only right to do the dishes after he had cooked such a lovely meal.

"That is not necessary." Mr. Conners started to grab the dishes away from Lennox's hands.

"It's the least I can do," Lennox smiled. She wanted to somehow show kindness to him for all the kindness he showed her.

Mr. Conners relinquished the dishes with a small smile. "Alright then." He returned to sipping his cup of hot tea.

Lennox placed the dishes in the sink's soapy water and grabbed the yellow sponge. Gazing out the kitchen window, she saw a bolt of lightning run across the sky as she scrubbed. A thunderstorm rolled in. Thunder crashed loud against the silence of the country and shook the foundations of the earth. The old home rumbled with every crash. Lennox loved to watch storms roll in. She sat on the back porch with her father and counted the seconds between the lightning and the thunder.

"Go on outside and enjoy the storm. It will help clear your mind. I will finish up." Mr. Conners rolled his chair forward to take Lennox's place at the old farm sink. He had watched her stare out the window while she scrubbed the same plate for minutes.

"I don't mind finishing them up," she said, insisting on finishing the last few dishes.

"I insist you go on outside and relax," Mr. Conners said, not taking "No" for an answer.

Lennox smiled and mouthed "Thank you" before she walked outside onto the porch.

Out in the country, Lennox appreciated the better view as the storm approached. The tall grass swayed like the ocean's waves. The leaves twirled in the wind as if dancing. The wind blew her hair into her face so she tucked the brown locks behind her ears. Lennox watched as God's creation shook before Him. She breathed in the fresh country air. Her spirit stirred as she tried to shake the continued feeling of heaviness. She wanted to break free like the lightning broke through the sky.

Without warning, the sound of two fighter jets soared over the country house. Lennox looked up just in time to see their silver silhouettes fly off into the distance. The noise could be mistaken for thunder if it weren't for the high-pitched screams that trailed at the end of their mighty roar.

Sky and his grandpa rushed outside, looked up at the dark clouds, and then to Lennox. Lennox's eyes were glued to the gray clouds above her.

"What was that?" Sky asked with eyebrows furrowed.

"It sounded like the fighter jets I used to fly when I was in the Air Force," Mr. Conners added.

"I think they *were* fighter jets," Lennox said, unsure of what she really saw.

Fighter jets that flew out this far made no sense. The nearest Air Force Base was over a city away. The only time she saw them was on the news, fighting in wars that she wanted no part of, and when her family went to air shows when she was smaller.

Mr. Conners bowed his head in prayer as if he knew what was happening, "Lord, give us strength."

Immediately, two more jets flew overhead… then another pair… and another. Lennox's body stiffened as if it was water that turned to ice. She agreed with the prayer, knowing she needed strength for the road ahead. Whatever it may be. She felt something big was about to happen. The tides would turn, but not for the better. God prepared them for something. She wished she knew what.

Chapter 12

Summer's heat and humidity fast approached as days passed. They did not see fighter jets in the sky and the news didn't report anything about them. In the back of Lennox's mind, she knew something happened. School administrators dismissed all classes and started summer break early "due to the prom attack." Could it really be because there were more attacks on the horizon? Thank God she and Sky acquired all of their credits to receive diplomas.

Time to search for answers was at Lennox's disposal. If she had the fortitude, she could go back to her house and scour every inch of every room for clues on how the Regime knew her parents—if they knew them at all. Her mind roamed and thought longer about the jets she had seen. They could have been nothing—she hoped they were nothing—but she knew they were everything.

The next several days returned to normal. There were only a few whispers and low murmurs about the jets that flew over a week ago.

After Sunday's church service, Sky and Mr. Conners had a surprise waiting for Lennox. It was her eighteenth birthday. A vanilla cake with buttercream icing and sprinkles waited for her on the kitchen table. She could tell it was homemade because of the imperfections, but that was the reason she loved it all the more.

"I thought everyone would have forgotten," Lennox said as the smile grew on her face. Although it was painful to celebrate a birthday for the first time without her parents, Kira, and Oliver's presence, she was still grateful Sky remembered.

"I can't forget my best friend's birthday," Sky said as he lit the two candles shaped like the numbers one and eight.

As Mr. Conners and Sky sang "Happy Birthday," Lennox remembered how close she came to not seeing eighteen. The raised scar on her chest that barely showed above her Sunday dress was a painful reminder of the school bombing and her loss, but now it also reminded her there was a reason she was still alive… there was a reason she survived. She had a purpose to serve. She would do whatever it took to fulfill it. At least, she hoped she would. She did not want to take the breath in her lungs for granted. Too many had lost theirs.

As she bent down to blow out the candles, she made a wish in her heart that felt more like a prayer, "Let me keep my faith, no matter what."

She blew.

Sky and Mr. Conners clapped their hands and shouted victoriously for Lennox's next year of life.

Mr. Conners opened the screened front door and rolled himself to the mailbox. He refused to let Lennox or Sky get the mail for him. He wheeled back with a stack of junk mail and bills, but one piece of mail stood out.

Lennox anticipated a letter from Oliver. He left messages via the personal hologram portal, but in his last message nearly a month ago, he gave Lennox a cryptic message that said he would handwrite her soon. Handwritten letters were rare and not practiced by her brother, which made Lennox somewhat concerned.

Mr. Conners sifted through the mail piece-by-piece. His fingers stopped on the one Lennox eyed.

"This one is for you," he said politely, handing it to Lennox.

She reached for it with a smile, "Thank you. I'm not sure why he chose to mail this one." She was glad to hear from him either way.

Lennox unsealed the pale envelope and slowly pulled the paper out to read its message. As she read further down the page, her smile faded to a frown.

"Is everything okay, dear?" Mr. Conners asked, looking at the paper Lennox held in her now trembling hands.

"Lennox, what is it?" Sky asked, walking closer to her. He knew her facial expressions.

"Uh, it's… it's a warning." Lennox's heart pounded so loudly in her chest she heard it in her ears.

"A warning?" Sky's facial features scrunched together as he shook his head.

Mr. Conners rolled his chair closer. "What does it say?"

"Oliver says that they are losing control of military bases. The Regime has infiltrated his training facility and probably others all over the world. He says there's a fracture in the ranks, and some of our own are siding with the Regime." The letter shook in Lennox's hands. Her heart raced as time stood still. "He said the Regime is going to start taking over entire cities and start building their own strongholds."

Lennox turned the letter over and saw more writing. She placed her hand on her chest where her mother's locket rested and found a chair to sit in. She could not stand after what she must read next. Her dad was not just a teacher and her mom was not merely a nurse. They were a part of an underground organization—the Sparrows—that fought for the rights of fellow believers in Christ. The Sparrows recently took a stand against the Regime in foreign countries. That was why her parents were killed, for their involvement with the Sparrows. She read further and her hand gripped tighter around the locket. Their murders were not random at all. She felt a sense of closure, but new questions swept in. Lennox was uncertain she could answer them.

"There's more," Lennox continued. She looked at Sky, and then to Mr. Conners. "Oliver is siding with the group known as 'the Sparrows.' He said my parents were a part of that group." Lennox noticed a suppressed reaction from Mr. Conners when she said "Sparrows."

She paused before she explained further. "He says that the locket my mother left me has a microchip that could help stop the Regime, and that I needed to take it to a place called 'Sparrow City' immediately."

Lennox was unsure she could fulfill this destiny, and her palms began to sweat. Why would her mother leave something so important with *her*? Lennox thought if anyone should have something of such value, it should be Oliver. He could get it to Sparrow City. Why her?

Lennox's racing mind shifted to Mr. Conners' sweet, endearing face. "Mr. Conners, he said you would know how to help."

Mr. Conners nodded with an open jaw. "I never thought I would live to see this day." He rested his elbow on the arm of his wheelchair and cupped his hand over his mouth.

"What day, Pop?" Sky asked.

"The birth of the American Underground Church." Mr. Conners rubbed his chin with his wrinkled hand and shook his head. "I have an old war buddy named Eli. You remember Eli, don't you, Sky? We would spend summers out at his cabin when you were a boy."

"Sort of, but what does Eli have to do with this?" Sky paced back and forth with his hands on top of his head trying to figure it all out. Lennox held her head in her hands and rubbed her forehead. It was all so hard to take in.

"He founded the Sparrows a very long time ago when he saw the persecution of Christians during our war days. He always told me this day was coming sooner than later. I never thought it would happen in my lifetime, though. The cabin is a safe house. You need to get Lennox out of here, before it's too late." Mr. Conners rolled his chair to a cabinet, pulled out a piece of paper, and scribbled down what was in his head. "The fighter jets flying overhead are only the beginning. It's not safe here anymore. These directions will take you to the cabin. Go straight there. Don't make any stops, do you understand?" Mr. Conners handed Sky the paper.

"What about you? If the Regime is taking over, I can't just leave you here." Sky crouched down and peered into his grandfather's blue eyes.

"Of course you can. I can take care of myself. I have a responsibility to be here and help others escape what lies before us. Besides, I will only slow you down and you can't afford that." He tapped the wheel of his chair. "The locket Lennox has is too valuable. She's not safe here."

Not safe here? Lennox held the locket between her fingers, clicking it open and shut and recited the verse in her head over and over. "We walk by faith, not by sight... we walk by faith, not by sight."

So this was it. This was her life now—a life no longer safe or sure. She felt as if the rug was jerked from under her feet. Everything happened too fast. She wasn't ready for it all to come crashing down. She was finally starting to mend.

What kind of microchip was implanted in a locket? Why did her mom trust her with something so valuable? It was too much all at once. Processing the information took up valuable time they did not have. Lennox felt the urgency in her soul, but the weakness of her flesh tried to take control. She knew she had to leave. She must try for her parents... for Kira... but Sky's house felt like home now. It required all she had to leave.

Chapter 13

Sky and Lennox drove for hours down the dark roads to the cabin when the truck got stuck in a patch of mud. They heard the sound of jets approaching over them while the truck stalled, reminding them of the importance to keep moving—and fast. Sky hit the gas pedal, but the tires sputtered in the mud.

"Oh, come on…" Sky moaned with frustration as he stomped harder on the pedal.

He gripped the steering wheel tighter and hit the gas pedal harder several more times. The tires spun without moving forward. "Lennox, take the wheel and rev the gas. I am going to get out and push."

Lennox slid into the driver's seat as her blood pulsed through her veins. She stomped on the gas. Lennox felt paranoid being out in the middle of nowhere, especially since she possessed a microchipped locket that had the capability to stop the Regime— the Regime that was taking over.

Sky groaned as he strained to push the truck out of the ditch. Mud slung up as Lennox slammed her foot on the pedal, touching it to the floorboard. Sky pushed with one last-ditch effort and freed the truck. Lennox slid back over to the passenger's seat as Sky jumped in on the driver's side. He wasted no time and pressed on the gas to get them out of the stale darkness. The truck twisted its way onto the road with mud splashing behind it.

"How much farther until we reach the cabin?" Lennox asked, looking at the map Mr. Conners drew. Her eyes wandered from the directions to Sky. His clothes were splattered with mud and his face was red. Sweat glued his black hair to his face.

"We should only be a few miles away," Sky said, taking a sharp turn into a heavily wooded area.

It reminded Lennox of the old, scary movies she hated to watch. There were no lights and no signs of life this far out in the country. It made her uneasy. The truck took them several more miles until it stopped in front of an old log cabin located next to a small pond.

"Stay here. Let me make sure it's safe first."

Sky left her where she was and made his way closer to the cabin. The hoot of an owl echoed and yellow eyes stared down at them.

"Can't we just go together?" Lennox whispered loudly from the truck when he was a few feet away. Everyone she loved was dead or off to war, except for Sky. All she wanted was to stay close.

"No, just wait here. Okay? And let me go first." Sky ended the conversation and made his way to the cabin. He had nothing to defend himself with except his own two fists. If there was a stranger inside, he was in trouble.

An older man with dark skin and a fresh white beard swung open the cabin door and stood threateningly on the first step.

"What do you want, boy?" he growled.

"Eli?" Sky tilted his head in question.

"Yes, that's me," the old man nodded. He was tall and muscular, which was surprising considering he looked about the same age as Sky's grandpa.

"My pop, Roger Conners, sent us here to find you. He says you can help us."

"You're Roger's boy?" Eli motioned Sky inside.

"Grandson. My name's Sky." Sky turned to wave Lennox over, but instead saw her standing five feet behind him. She had refused to stay in the truck as ordered. He was furious.

This was one of the few times Lennox saw his anger

plainly. In her mind, she couldn't let him walk into the cabin alone. There were just too many variables. Lennox didn't know what she would do if the old man had turned on Sky, but at least she would be with him. It was better to stick together, she thought.

Lennox walked up three wooden steps and passed the cabin's threshold. The interior smelled like pine and dust. The dim lighting illuminated rustic furniture with Aztec print fabric. Only one lamp was on. Sky followed Eli inside. He turned around to offer them a seat, but noticed Lennox's necklace instead.

"Where'd you get that?"

"My mother. It's why we are here." Lennox covered the locket with her hand. She would guard whatever it held, no matter how much she wanted to give it to someone more capable of protecting it. There must be a reason her mom trusted it to her.

Sky jumped in. "She got a letter from her brother— who is in the military—saying that her parents were killed because of their involvement in a group known as the Sparrows. Now she has this necklace that her mother gave her. It has a microchip in it that can stop the Regime somehow. My Pop says you founded the Sparrows, and can help us get to Sparrow City."

The deep wrinkles carved into Eli's face faded to his forehead as he raised his eyebrows. "Your mother is Cadence Winters, and your father is Haiden Winters?"

"Yes, that's right. You know them?" Lennox asked, intrigued by how he knew them—or rather—*had* known them. Of course, he would know them, seeing as he was the Head of the Sparrows. She wished her parents had told her of their involvement in the first place. It would have kept her from such a surprise after their deaths.

"Yes, they were wonderful people. I am very sorry for your loss. You should know your parents are heroes. They gave their lives for others. They were helping to fund underground churches all over the world. We call it 'Operation Sparrow.'" Eli locked his dark brown eyes to Lennox's.

Her anger and sorrow twisted with a hint of pride. She should have known they died for a cause. She had no idea her parents were involved in such an operation and could not figure out why they did not tell her. Maybe it was for her safety? Of course it was.

Now she knew why they were murdered. She should feel comforted, but it was still hard to accept the fact they were really gone. She chose to let this knowledge drive her to do what was right. She wanted to continue what they had started, and maybe, make a difference like they had.

"We have been tracking the movements of the Regime for quite a while," Eli continued. "They have slowly taken over several foreign nations, and we knew it was only a matter of time before they reached here." Eli shook his head. "There is a man named Ahab, who is the Commander of the Regime. Ever since he rose to power, he has been targeting Christian countries and turning them into Regime strongholds."

"How can he do that? Can no one stop him?" Sky asked.

"He has numbers—soldiers that will do anything for him at whatever cost. They've assembled a weapon that can control the weather. It's called the 'Global Weather Simulator.' It is the fiercest weapon I have ever seen. He has already destroyed hundreds of defiant cities with it."

"Why haven't we heard any of this on the news?" Lennox asked.

"I can only suspect they did not want to start a public panic or mass hysteria. There is already enough civil unrest. The government is barely holding the states together as it is." Eli reached for a tablet and pressed play. "One minute the land seems fine, and then the next—terrible extremes. They have already demolished thousands of acres and have destroyed entire cities with fires, tornadoes, hurricanes, and tsunamis. See for yourself…" Eli held out the small tech screen for their observation.

Sky stood over Lennox's shoulder as they both watched in horror. The Regime plagued the countries that would not surrender with what they called "acts of God." Hundreds of thousands were left without aide—their houses washed away by floods, and their crops destroyed by wildfires. People soon became climate refugees. Lennox would never forget what she watched. The voices crying out for help echoed in her ears. She wanted to help them, but she could do nothing. She hated the helpless sensation that invaded the depths of her soul.

"Is there any way to disable it?" Lennox asked, handing the screen back to Eli.

"Your locket." Eli smiled and pointed to the sparrow around Lennox's neck. "Your father was working on something that would bring down the Regime. I believe he hid it in a microchip… in *that* locket. That is why you must get it to Sparrow City."

Lennox remembered walking into the garage where her father spent long hours. She recalled his diligence as he worked on something, but could not remember what it was. It all began to make a little more sense. Why did she not think of this before? Why would her father and mother work so hard on something, only to leave it with her? Was there no one else who could get it to Sparrow City? She trembled with uncertainty. Was she even capable of getting the microchip to Sparrow City?

Lennox, you can do this. You have to.

The necklace weighed heavily around her neck. As much as she wanted to hand the burden over to someone else, deep down she knew it was her responsibility. It was her course to take and her burden to bear.

Eli folded his hands together as he sat down on the rustic chair behind him. "There is no doubt the Regime has already set up strongholds, and I'm sure they are targeting areas with the GWS. You have to get that microchip to Sparrow City. The only safe way there for you and the locket is by foot, but you will never survive without gear."

Lennox's head hurt from all of the information and her pulse sped up. Eli scratched his head and breathed heavily. "You need to stop at a Sparrow outpost. My daughter, Cameron, is at one about fifteen miles from here and will give you everything you need."

Eli stood back up, unable to sit as he spoke further. "You should know that this man, Ahab, thinks he is a god. He is making everyone bow to him and denounce whatever other faith they are. He has an anthem that plays every day at 7 a.m. and 7 p.m. where he makes every man, woman, and child bow to him. He will show no mercy to those who refuse to follow his command."

Eli held out the screen again. Hundreds of men, women, and children moved as a song played loudly in the air. They moved like moths to a flame and all bowed. One woman stood and refused to bow like the rest, and that is when Lennox saw the price of not bowing. Regime soldiers hit the woman in the back of the knees and forced her to bow. When she fought to get back up, they ended it. Ended her. Tears fell down Lennox's cheeks as she felt her faith waver.

No, Lennox. You have to keep the faith. Faith in Christ is worth it… always.

She thought back to the released video of her parents and how they never wavered. Wiping the tears away, she sat down on the dusty sofa and wondered about what the world had become. How were they going to prevail against such a force? How would she be strong enough? She felt so unprepared for everything. She wanted time to stand still until she figured it all out. But time did what it did best—it pressed forward. She must do the same.

Eli spoke up again as if he read Lennox's inner questions. "You will be safe when you get to Sparrow City. The Sparrows have been building it for a long time now, anticipating this would happen. There is a team of scientists who have built up tech to withstand the GWS and attacks from the Regime. It is a city of refuge for all who can make it there."

All she had to do was make it to Sparrow City. She would do everything in her power to get there.

The sun's rays broke through the cabin's windows, illuminating the dust particles that filled the room. After much-needed rest, Sky and Lennox woke up to Eli scrambling eggs. Eli brought a plate of eggs to both of them. As they ate at the small kitchen table, Eli's eyes grew serious and his voice stern in an oddly uplifting way.

"You two be careful when you leave to head to the Sparrow outpost, there are dangerous men out here. The Regime has spies everywhere."

Sky and Lennox nodded their heads with understanding. Lennox swallowed hard and bit her bottom lip for distraction. She could not think of everything without becoming overwhelmed or wanting to turn back—which was not an option.

Eli put one arm around Sky and the other around Lennox as he sat between them. "I know you are young, but you need to know when you serve God, to live is gain and to die is gain. Don't let fear of the Regime overtake you. Don't give them power over your faith."

Lennox's heart thumped inside her chest as her faith was challenged. She wanted freedom from fear's persuasion, but fear was all she felt. Being on the run and leaving everything behind tested her more than she expected. She knew in advance it was hard, but didn't realize how afraid it would make her. She felt like every part of her was unstable.

Chapter 14

Lennox watched as the small trail that led to the cabin faded beneath her feet. She looked back and waved goodbye to Eli. She hoped that one day she would see him again—that she would come out of this alive.

"You ready?" Sky asked ten feet ahead of her.

"Ready."

She pulled her satchel from the truck and slung it over her head as she ran to catch up with him.. Sky held out the compass that Eli gave him and headed due north— the direction Eli said the Sparrow outpost was. Lennox followed close behind, making sure not to stray too far from Sky's side. She wished they could take the truck, but the forest grew too dense the deeper they went. There was no way a truck could maneuver through the trees.

They walked for so long that Lennox felt blisters form on her feet. She focused on the back of Sky's head, trying to keep her thoughts from the pain. She focused on Oliver and Kira as she hustled to match Sky's pace. She wanted to go back to normal so badly that she clearly heard each one of their voices in her head, urging her to move forward.

With every step, the dirt and branches crunched beneath their weight. Sky walked louder than he realized. The wind howled and made a piercing noise through the trees. Lennox was grateful for the whistling wind. It helped cover their tracks and masked the noises they made as Sky tromped over the dry earth beneath them. Lennox wondered how the earth transitioned so quickly from pasty mud to cracked dirt that resembled a barren desert. She had not fully realized how unstable the GWS made the climate. It disrupted the entire atmosphere.

The wind died down and a twig snapped loudly. She knew someone close enough could hear them trample through the woods. They both paused in fear, hesitating to move again. There could be danger anywhere. Lennox looked around but did not see—or hear—any movement except for their own.

Just over fifteen miles later, they reached the Sparrow outpost where their welcome was anything but warm. Five soldiers in steel-gray uniforms with sparrows on their sleeves ran out from behind the bushes and pointed strange weapons at Sky and Lennox.

"Stop right there!" yelled a stout soldier with broad shoulders.

They lifted their hands in the air.

"Eli sent us. My name is Sky, and this is Lennox." Sky showed them the compass with an engraved sparrow and Eli's initials—*E.J.*—on the back.

A tall, slender woman with high cheekbones and feminine features removed herself from a large camouflage tent. Her hair was a pile of braids wrapped in a bun on top of her head. The closer she walked, the more her features resembled Eli's.

"You said Eli sent you?" She narrowed her dark eyes and reached for the compass. "Weapons down!" The Sparrows obeyed her command and lowered their weapons. "I'm Cameron. Eli is my father. If he sent you to us instead of straight to Sparrow City, you must be important." Cameron handed the compass back to Sky.

"Her locket is." Sky pointed to Lennox, but stood protectively in front of her.

Lennox stepped out from behind him and lifted the locket up for Cameron to see.

"That *is* very important. My father spoke about that

locket." Cameron motioned them to follow her to her camouflage tent.

Inside, Lennox saw more men and women in steel-gray uniforms. Some were awake and played cards while others were fast asleep. A few were badly injured. Some had a strange scar on their left arm, visible only because they rolled up their dark gray sleeves. Cameron saw the concerned questions that grew inside Lennox—she hid her thoughts poorly.

"The Regime is closer than before and starting to build strongholds all over the world, including very close to here," Cameron explained. "We have been fighting for a long time trying to dismantle the Regime."

Again, Lennox caught herself staring at the strange scar and tried to look away, but couldn't. She grabbed her own arm defensively. "What about the scar on their left arm?"

Lennox hoped she wasn't being too forward or insensitive, but she had to know. She could tell that it came from an abnormal injury. Would *that* be her fate? She wanted as much information as Cameron would give.

Cameron rolled up her sleeve and exposed the raised, silver colored scar on the inside of her dark skinned arm.

It was D-shaped. "This is the price of being captured. The Regime calls it branding, *D* for Defier."

Now Lennox clearly saw the *D* encased in a circle on their arms. She bit the inside of her cheek like Oliver did growing up.

"How...why..." Lennox had so many more questions. This was not her world. It couldn't be. Her thoughts swam in circles in her head.

"If they choose to let you live when they capture you, they mark you with a "D" to show that you are "Defiant" and that you refuse to give up your faith in Christ. On the outskirts of every Regime stronghold, they have prisoner camps where they keep all of the people who refuse to bow during the anthem. That is where they brand them. We were lucky enough to escape the prison with only a scar."

Lennox vividly remembered the song that played on the tech screen as she watched the woman refuse to bow. Her body was dragged away into the darkness like she was nothing. Lennox cringed.

Cameron shook her head and continued, "Sometimes the scar is left by branding irons that they used to use to brand cattle. If you are not so lucky, they carve it into your skin with a dull knife."

A lump formed in Lennox's throat. The thought of being captured terrified her. Her heart felt compassion for the Sparrows who went through so much. Then it hit her. This was why her parents supported the Sparrows. They tried to give people hope that it was possible to resist the Regime. It was possible not to bow. They tried to make a way for others to escape. Lennox wished they were there so they could tell her what to do.

"That is why it is so important that you get that microchip to Sparrow City. It can change everything." Cameron let out a heavy sigh. "I would take it myself if there wasn't another mission I had been tasked with. I can't afford to lose any manpower to help you. The mission my crew is tasked with is also too important to fail. You two are going to have to get it there by yourselves. Besides, they will never suspect two teenagers. You two probably have the best chance of getting it there fastest."

Lennox lowered her head. She hoped they would at least be able to escort her and Sky to Sparrow City.

Cameron walked to a red traveling trunk with a white sparrow painted on its lid and unlatched the lock. Pulling out several things, she walked back to where Sky and Lennox stood.

"Here is a pack with survival gear and a first aid kit, should you need it. I put MREs—meals ready to eat—in there as well. You can't eat city food. They started to put micro trackers in them that will alert them if someone tries to leave the city." Handing the pack to Sky, she held up another item that looked like a silver baton. "This is a Sapphire Shield. It can withstand a firing squad."

Lennox never wanted to put that to the test.

Cameron pushed a button on the baton and a crystal clear material formed into the shape of a strong sphere. She pushed the button again and it retracted back into a baton. Cameron shoved it into the bag.

"These might be the most important," Cameron said, handing both Lennox and Sky a package. "They are all-terrain suits and will protect you from the harsh elements caused by the GWS. That thing has got everything out of whack."

"This will protect us from the extremes?" Sky asked holding up the package containing a silver jumpsuit and boots.

"Yes, it will. It keeps you cool in the desert climates and warm in the frozen climates. They will do nothing for you should a tornado, earthquake, or flash flood come, though. So I hope you have good instincts. You can put them on over your clothes."

Lennox thought she was joking at first, but it was no joke. The suits kept them comfortable in extreme temperatures, but could do nothing for them if they were swept away by water or tornado winds. Lennox broke the seal to the plastic box. The all-terrain suit was neatly packaged inside. As she pulled it out, piece by piece, it reminded her of what astronauts used to wear, just not as bulky. It had a metallic silver color to it with the red Sparrow symbol on both sleeves. She put it on over her clothes and found she actually moved comfortably in it.

"Just make sure the helmet guard is activated and sealed properly. It will form over your face like a second skin and protect your face from the elements," Cameron said as she activated Sky's.

Lennox saw the tech form over his face. It was amazing technology that she did not know existed.

"One more thing." Cameron came forward and handed Sky and Lennox a strange looking knife, "It's an adapter blade. Its molecular structure is designed to change to the exact tool you need when you need it."

This was not how Lennox expected to end her last summer vacation. Tech suits, shields, and adapter blades reminded her just how quickly and significantly her world changed. It was as if she watched someone else's life unfold. She felt like she saw a movie instead of reality.

Cameron sighed as she stared at the dirt. She lifted her chin and met their eyes. "I have to warn you that your trek will not be easy. The route on the map I am giving you is the safest way to bring the locket to Sparrow City. It is plagued by many things. You must first climb straight up the center of the Guadalupe Mountains where the weather is being manipulated by the GWS. There are sleeping drones at the east and west of it. If you try to bypass it and go around you will wake them up and the Regime will find you, or worse, the drones will drop bombs directly on you." Cameron looked at Sky and Lennox intensely, making sure they absorbed the information she gave them. "And then there are Prowlers."

"Prowlers?" Lennox clasped the locket in her fist.

"Prowlers are the result of a science experiment that Ahab ran. Their strength is not their greatest weapon, although they are strong. It is the psychological warfare they can play from a distance." Cameron stiffened and rubbed her jaw with her hand. "They do not have to be right next to you to destroy you. If anyone crosses the line into their territory, the mind game will begin. If you cross the line into their territory, they will try to steal your soul. They can only hold on to one person's mind at a time and can only stray so far from their territory, but don't underestimate them."

"How can they steal my soul?" Lennox pondered silently. She could not fathom such a creature. She folded into herself at the thought of such a being. She still tried to fully grasp what the world had become. It seemed so unreal. Normalcy unraveled and gave way to chaos and uncertainty.

Ear-piercing sirens raged through the airwaves. Lennox's first thought was tornadoes. She heard tornado sirens years ago when terrible storms pummeled through the fields not too far from her house.

"Tornado sirens?" Sky asked Cameron, thinking the same as Lennox.

Cameron looked at him with the intensity of a hunting lion. "War sirens. The government had them put in after the last civil disturbance. The outbreak of civilians fighting against themselves made the sirens necessary.

Sparrows must have commandeered them. There is a military base ten minutes away in Cordova. They must have sounded the sirens from there." Cameron hastily gathered supplies and handed everything to Sky. "Get her out of here, now!"

Sparrows grabbed their weapons and loaded into trucks. Lennox looked at Sky, shaking her head in disbelief.

"Now!" Cameron urged. She shoved Lennox and Sky out of the tent, commanding their feet to hurry.

Midday was never so bleak.

Chapter 15

Leaving the safety of the Sparrows put Lennox's senses on high alert. She heard every leaf move and saw every branch shake. She was intensely aware of her surroundings and knew they could change at any minute. They could not afford to be careless about their movements—or about anything, anymore. Lennox thought back to when she and Sky were little and everything was fine. They played hide and seek in woods similar to the ones they were in now—it was a much different kind of hide and seek now.

They were less than thirty miles away from the Sparrow outpost when the terrain shifted from forest to desert. Foliage vanished and the ground transformed into dirt and rubble. It looked as if someone drew a straight line in the dirt and told the trees not to pass. The broken up cement and rebar were the only ruins that remained.

Lennox and Sky stepped out from the cover of the dense tree line and felt the suit work its magic. The sun shined brighter than Lennox ever saw before. A tinted guard on her helmet automatically shielded her eyes from the harsh light. The censors in the suits registered their body temperatures and displayed them on the screens of their helmets.

"Did you know they did that?" Lennox asked Sky in amazement. She was unaware of how advanced technology had become.

"I had no idea… not only does it register our temperatures, but our vitals as well. I have never seen anything like it," Sky said as he read his vitals.

These suits were more than amazing—they were a godsend. If they encountered the weather they saw on the video, they needed all the advantages they could get.

Lennox looked down to check the soles of her boots. They were good too. She was certain the rubber soles of their old boots would melt within minutes in this extreme heat, but with gear like this, they could survive as long as it did, and as long as nothing more intense came their way.

They moved through the desert terrain with weary feet, but at least the suits felt like they had air-conditioners blasting to keep them cool. The only drawback to this desert terrain was that there was no cover to hide if they ran into Regime soldiers. Cameron told them drones did not usually come out to this location on the map, but Lennox still could not shake the feeling that drones followed them. If there were Regime soldiers, then what? Soldiers could spot them before Lennox and Sky even knew they were there. Lennox did not want to think of what the Regime would do if they were caught with this kind of gear. She thought of the terrible scars left on the Sparrows' arms and shuddered.

No, I won't be afraid.

She did not want to let fear rule her, but that was all she felt. She chose not to wallow in fear and shook off the feeling as much as she could. She must hold on to the hope that if anyone did see them, they would mistake them for mirages caused by the sweltering heat.

Lennox followed directly behind Sky.

One of their monitors triggered an alarm in their suits. A message flashed across the screens of their helmets that read "WARNING EXTREME FATIGUE."

They traveled for well over eight hours. Lennox figured their drive to reach safety kept them going without truly feeling the toll it took on their bodies. She paid little attention to her body before the alarm, but now she felt the weariness in her muscles. They ached and twitched from the endless hours of walking. She glanced at Sky, wondering if he felt it too. His eyes revealed that he did.

"Let's take a break and eat. We can rest for an hour, at most," Sky said.

Lennox knew it strained him to stop, even for an hour. If it weren't for her, he would probably keep going. She hated the fact she weighed him down.

Lennox's legs collapsed under her as she nodded in agreement. It felt good to sit down.

They covered a lot of ground and still, the majority of the day remained for their journey to the map's designated campsite. The directions they got from Cameron at the outpost were specific on where to set up camp. The Sparrows probably possessed more inside information about the Regime's routines than Lennox ever imagined.

"What are our choices?" Lennox asked, pointing to the MREs. She never ate one before.

"Well, let's see here… we have chili macaroni, or vegetable lasagna. You choose which one you want. They will have to sustain us for a while. It looks like the only food we have." He waved both options in the air.

"I am going to have to go with the vegetable lasagna, no contest," Lennox said.

"Really? I thought for sure you were going to go with the chili again," Sky laughed at his reference to the last time she ate chili—when she got sick.

"You're hilarious," she rolled her eyes. At least he tried to keep the mood light. Lennox still worried about it being the only food they had. She never expected uncertainty in regards where their next meal came from.

Sky tossed her the lasagna and deactivated his helmet so he could eat his chili macaroni. He kept his head down to avoid exposing his skin to the sun that scorched the ground with its heat. Lennox looked down at her dinner's brown package. She was reminded to be thankful she was not going to starve to death just yet. She tore open the package and ate its contents.

"You know this vegetable lasagna is not half bad," she mumbled with her head down. "It is probably just as good as that lasagna I made you and Oliver years ago. Do you remember that? I was so excited to make you all a big dinner."

"How could I forget? You almost burned down the entire kitchen in the process."

"Hey, give me a break. I was like eleven when that happened." Lennox shook her head at her eleven-year-old self.

"Those were some good days, weren't they?" Sky strained his eyes to look at her.

"Yeah, they really were. I wish things were like they used to be."

Lennox's heart yearned to be back home, safe with her mom and dad. But that was not meant to be. *This* life was her fate. No matter how many days, weeks, or years would pass, she always relished the good memories, but she knew she could not stay and live in them. She had to move on and keep moving forward.

Sky handed her the water pouch and she drank the last drop. The water soothed her chapped lips. They went through their water supply too fast, though they did not have much to start with. They needed to learn how to ration.

"We will need to find a water source soon," she said, holding up the pouch.

Lennox reactivated the tech around her face and made sure it sealed properly with the interlock so she could look at Sky. He was already done and had his helmet guard reactivated.

"My water pouch is dry too," he replied. "Our next stop shows that there is a stream where we can fill them up, unless that has turned into desert as well." He pulled out the map so they both could determine the chances the stream was still there. Neither one of them knew what to expect from the GWS.

"See, we are right here," Sky said, pointing to their place on the map. He was always good with directions. "If we can make it another few miles before sunset, we will have enough light to search the area for water. Hopefully, this stream still exists and we won't have to search that hard."

"Sounds good. Just a few more minutes and I will be ready to go," Lennox said, willing herself to get up. Her body said "Stop, or at the least slow down," but she knew she couldn't.

The hour of rest felt like seconds, and hours of trekking felt like days. Fifteen miles was nothing compared to the distance they needed to travel. They followed the compass' direction, hoping the earth's magnetic field had not changed. If they waited to travel by night, they would at least have the stars, but in the desert sun's glare they barely saw with their shields on. Maybe it was a better idea to wait.

Hour after hour passed by. Sky and Lennox were unusually silent. Lennox was sure Sky was as lost in his own thoughts as she was in hers. They were comfortable in each other's silence, and Lennox appreciated that.

They moved at an even pace side-by-side. Out of nowhere, the dirt swirled around them and small pebbles of ice fell from the sky, clinking against their helmets. As soon as the ice hit the ground it melted.

"Well, here is our water source." Sky collected small pellets of ice in his pouch.

Lennox did the same. "This is bizarre," she said as she watched the freezing, white ice fall from the darkening sky.

The pellets of ice grew to the size of quarters and the gusting wind was enough to make them walk sideways. Pushing against the wind, they struggled to walk forward.

"If they get any bigger we are going to have to take cover," Sky warned.

"Where?" Lennox asked, reminding him there was no cover.

Sky pulled out the Sapphire Shield Cameron gave

them and it formed in a perfect circle, "This should work, but let's keep moving forward as long as we can."

"Okay." Lennox squeezed close to Sky to get under the shield he held over their heads.

The hail was now the size of golf balls that fell at a rapid pace. They got pelted... hard. Every piece of hail felt like a bullet through their suits. They would have plenty of bruises when this was all over. They tried to walk close together, using the shield as one would use an umbrella against rain, but the hail seemed like it caught every gust of wind and flew from all directions straight into them. Staying low, they decided to cover themselves with as much of the shield as they could until the worst of it was over. The shield threatened to blow out of their hands. The gusts of wind almost defied gravity. Sky protected Lennox with his body and held the shield tightly over her so nothing hit her. Lennox was certain his exposed back was being beaten by the ice, but he never complained.

The ground must have cooled off enough for the ice to stick, because the barren desert turned white. The sound of the ice hitting the shield sounded like rain hitting a tin roof.

Clink, clink, clink.

It was almost tolerable. It reminded Lennox of hailstorms she watched with her dad until the hail got too big.

The golf ball-sized ice turned into boulder-sized ice within minutes. It would crush them if they were unable to hold the shield in place. Lennox helped Sky hold the shield above them with all of her strength, but the velocity at which the hail fell was impossible to withstand. The ice boulders crashed to the ground and splintered as they hit. Shards of ice buried themselves like daggers into the earth. If one landed directly on top of them, it would break both of their arms and smash them as if they were mere ants.

"What do we do?" Lennox asked. She prayed silently while waiting for Sky's reply.

"Be patient, it will be over soon," he said. Lennox hoped he was right.

"How do you know?" she asked.

"Because, I can see a break in the horizon," he reassured her, nodding toward the eastern sky.

Hail still fell all around them. The chances the hailstorm would end before a boulder-sized piece of ice fell on them seemed slim. Lennox waited for an eternity before she looked up. She saw the sky just east of them lose its darkness and turn to an iridescent pink and orange haze.

The hailstorm was over, its only evidence was the ice it left behind. The ice looked like delicate, frozen crystals protruding from the ground like beautiful, deadly diamonds.

"How cold do you think it is? Look at the hail… it is not melting at all," Lennox wondered.

Sky pressed the outer thermal censor of his suit. "The suit's censor says it is zero degrees Fahrenheit." He paced back and forth, crunching the ice beneath him. How much worse would it get? How could the GWS possibly turn the Texas summer into northern winter weather? He bit his bottom lip and furrowed his eyebrows. "Lennox, we have to make it to camp soon. I don't think my body can take another beating like that again soon."

Lennox agreed. "Okay, if we pick up the pace a little to make up for the hail storm, we can make it to a safe resting place. We are only a few more miles away from where the map says to make camp," she said, wanting to do whatever he needed her to do. She felt bad that his body took the brunt of the hail. His ribs must be covered with bruises. Just as she finished speaking, she saw a flash of silver out of the corner of her eye. "Did you see that?" she motioned to Sky, her thoughts full of drones and Prowlers.

"I did. It's probably nothing. Let's just go. Let's keep moving." Sky walked faster through the terrain.

How could he say it was probably nothing? They were being followed, Lennox was sure of it.

They were uneasy the rest of the way and constantly looked over their shoulders to see if the silver flash followed them. Lennox knew it did. She just did not know who—or what—it was.

Chapter 16

After a full night's rest, they continued to Sparrow City. Time was a commodity they could not afford to waste. Several hours of walking brought them within a mile of the mountains. They made good time. It did not take them a full day to reach the mountains, like Lennox expected. They stayed dead center with the tallest peak in the group of jagged rocks that aligned perfectly north, careful not to stray to the east or west. They took Cameron's precautions about the sleeping drones seriously.

The closer they got to the base of the mountain's cliffs the more they tried to hide behind anything they could as they walked at a steady pace. Cement barricades and sandbags were placed by the former residents of this region to shelter the city from the Simulator. It was a nice try, but their attempts failed. The city was destroyed like all of the other defiant cities Lennox saw on the screen, and she wondered how many more cities would suffer the same fate. Why didn't they know about what happened here sooner? Did it all really happen that quickly?

The sun disappeared behind the mountains by the time they made it to its base. Lennox looked up at the night as the sun tucked away. She gasped as colors danced above her. Greens and blues did pirouettes on the snow-capped peaks. Sky reached for her hand and laced his fingers around hers. It was as beautiful as it was out of place. The unlikely aurora reminded Lennox of the rainbow God showed to Noah in the Bible. Maybe this was a promise to them—a promise they would make it to Sparrow City.

Lennox glanced at Sky. He was in just as much awe as she was. Nature's stunning display mesmerized the both of them. Sky's gaze drifted away from the night sky and rested on Lennox. It had been a long time since she saw a genuine smile from him, dimples and all. She knew he missed his grandfather, and not knowing where his dad was weighed heavily on his heart.

"Do you think this is a sign?" she asked, meeting his gaze.

"What? The aurora? Yeah, I do. This has to be a sign

to give hope to those traveling to Sparrow City. It's a symbol of hope if I ever saw one," Sky said with reinforced faith.

Lennox wanted to reinforce her own and took a moment to thank God for the sign she was sure He was giving them.

"Why do you think there are no drones in the center of the mountain?" Sky asked.

"Maybe it's because it's the highest part. Maybe they assume that no one could climb it successfully," Lennox said, straining her neck to see the peak. Heights did not bother her much, but looking up at the rock's crest filled her with an unexpected wave of doubt.

Cameron would have warned them of additional threats if she knew of them. Lennox was confident that they could climb it. She had no reason to doubt her. The only other thing she warned them about was Prowlers, but they did not see any sign of them out here. All Lennox knew for certain, was that they had to go this route. There was no other option except up and over. They must take their chances with the mountain to avoid the drones. They covered their tracks in case drones or soldiers ventured nearby. They could not risk anyone knowing they were on the mountain.

Lennox kept her dad's satchel. She knew it was impractical to climb with, but she could not bear to part with it. It held a change of clothes, an old family photograph, her Bible, and the map. Sky carried what was left of their already diminishing supplies and his sketchbook, which was more important to him than he let on. He often sketched when they rested. Lennox liked seeing how calm he was when he drew.

They secured their suits and attached the utility belts they were given around their waists. Neither knew if they did it the right way. Other than the small diving cliffs by the lake they frequented every summer, they had never climbed anything before.

The gear would be their greatest ally during the climb. They grabbed all of the rope from the pack Cameron shoved to Sky and tethered themselves together. They worked their way up the base of the mountain one step at a time.

The terrain was not steep and felt more like a hike. The snow and ice did not stick too much on the lower level of the mountain. It was strange to see snow in Texas during the summer. It made Lennox think about how strong the Regime's tech was. She hoped her locket had the power to fully shut down the Regime's weapons.

She did not want anyone else to lose their life.

Crevices and ledges appeared as they climbed. They were wide enough to walk up and easy to grab hold of without much struggle. Lennox and Sky's vitals looked good as they kept a faster pace than Lennox had anticipated. If they kept going at this rate, they would be over the peak within hours.

The wind pushed them back the higher they inched. The ice crept down the mountain to where they were and snow flurries wisped around them. Their course was now a climb, but still not as bad as Lennox thought it would be. It could be worse.

The spikes hidden in the soles of their boots shot out. Sky and Lennox tested the limits of their strength as they dug them into the mountain with force. Sky's hands grabbed the massive rock first, followed by Lennox. They moved slower now and triggered their suit's warnings. Their breathing was labored and their bodies weary.

"We are about to lose spaces to grab hold of," Sky shouted over the wind and snow. His breaths were short, but he continued, "We are going to need our adaptor blades. They will turn into the ice picks we need. *I hope.*"

He dug his spikes further into the rising earth. He reached into his belt to unlatch the blade while he held on with one hand. He slung it through the air with great force and it adapted into the sharp ice pick he needed. It slammed into the side of the mountain, holding Sky's weight with ease. Now, it was Lennox's turn.

She dug her spikes in just as he did and secured her body weight. She clung to the rock above her as tight as her fingers would cling and let go with her other to reach for the blade latched to her belt. As soon as she let go, she felt her body slip. One hand was not enough to hold her. With the colors still dancing in the night, she fell farther and farther down. The rope that tethered her to Sky was unraveling. Seconds more and the rope would run out and she would pull Sky right down with her. As she slid down the mountain, she scrambled to grab hold of something… anything.

Her body bounced down the jagged edges of the steep rock. The fibers of her suit could not withstand the blows. She wanted to scream, but she couldn't find her voice. Through the chaos, she heard Sky yell, "The blade, grab your blade!" She fumbled through the gear on her belt and found it. She unlatched it and slung it toward the icy rock. It caught, but not well enough. She still slid with both hands wrapped around the handle. Her mind was occupied with the upper half of her body when she should focus on the bottom half.

Through groans and with everything in her, she commanded her legs to be firm and her feet to be strong as she hurled them into the ice one at a time and regained stability just in the nick of time. The rope was a mere foot from being completely unraveled. She took a deep breath to regain her composure and held her position for a few moments before she resumed climbing. She'd lost a lot of distance.

She yelled up to Sky—who looked like he was about to backtrack to come get her—"Don't come get me. I'm fine. I will be right there." She hated the fact that she fell so far and almost cost them their lives.

All Sky could do was wait for her as she climbed her way back up to him. This time, she made sure her feet were anchored before she released a hand to sling the ice pick. Her suit was torn. Blood ran down her knees and arms from hitting the jagged edges as she fell. The cold wiggled its way up through her suit, making her shiver.

Her teeth chattered as if trying to break away the ice growing on her bones.

"That was a close call. Are you really okay?" Sky was genuinely concerned.

She could tell if she gave the word, he would forgo the rest of the climb and head back down only to do this all over again in the morning.

"I'm fine, really." She really was fine—for the most part—and did not think she had any broken bones. Her bloody legs and arms were not that bad. The scrapes did not feel that deep. She knew neither one of them could afford another slip like that.

Push yourself, Lennox.

She ignored the icy cold that she felt through her torn suit and kept climbing. They inched their way up higher and higher. They were only ten feet from the peak. There was a wide plateau big enough for two or three grown men to sit comfortably. Sky pulled himself on it and knelt down with an outstretched arm to help pull Lennox up. She reached up and met his grasp. He swung her onto the plateau, making sure she had her balance before he let go.

"You're bleeding," Sky said, raising his hand to her brow.

"It's nothing, really. I'm okay."

"No, you're not. You are probably freezing! Why didn't you tell me your suit was torn?" He took inventory of every rip in her suit and every scrape on her limbs. She was lucky none of her vital organs were punctured. Her suit still read her vitals and calculated the damage done. The suit made vigorous efforts to regulate her body temperature despite the holes.

"Good news is, my satchel made it," Lennox said, holding it up as if it were a trophy. She was trying to be positive.

"You and that satchel." Sky shook his head.

He took special interest in a gash on her forehead she didn't know she had. She must have ripped through the force field on her helmet as well.

"You need stitches. You're lucky your helmet repaired itself... too bad your head can't repair itself. You are going to have to switch off your helmet for a little while. I think the first aid kit Cameron gave us has a needle and thread in it," he said as he rummaged through his pack. "Yep, here it is." He threaded the needle with light from his headlamp, which could not have been easy. "Sorry, no anesthetics." He bit his lip and shook his head.

"It's okay, I'm ready." This would make her stronger.

Sky gently touched her forehead and sewed her skin back together by weaving the needle in and out. There was a sting every time the needle went through her skin, but it was not unbearable. He tied a knot at the end of the thread and cut the excess off.

"Five stitches. Not too bad. You just might have a little scar," he said.

"Thank you." She could not say anything else. She was just thankful she did not have to do this all alone.

"Do you think you can keep going?"

"Yeah, of course." She would keep going no matter what.

She had to.

Chapter 17

Lennox's feet were the first to drop on the other side of the mountain. Sky's feet soon followed. The spikes retracted into the soles of their boots. They reached the bottom of the mountain with more ease than when they scaled to the top. Lennox looked around. There were no drones visible. They had not set them off.

"We made it!" Sky picked up Lennox and spun her around. He squeezed her so tight the air to her lungs was cut off. He paused a moment and set her back down.

Her feet hugged the flat surface of the earth. She never thought she would be so happy to be on level ground again. She was glad to have one less obstacle standing between them and Sparrow City.

This side of the mountain's landscape was less barren. They saw forms of life sprouting from the earth. Rubble still encompassed them for the most part, but the spark of life could not be ignored. Lennox learned that life always found a way to break through. Life would not be denied. It pushed to survive, and that was exactly what they had to do.

Lennox was scanning her surroundings when the moon and stars blew out and it grew dark. The aurora disappeared and her vision turned hazy. Her feet were locked into place as if glued to the ground. She had no control over her body.

A Prowler.

Lennox had prayed this day would not come. Now she knew why the Regime didn't need to station soldiers here. She would rather face one hundred soldiers than one Prowler.

He stared straight at her with his reptilian eyes. One lone Prowler— not quite human, but not quite beast either. He had the face and shape of a man, but he was something different altogether. Lennox lost track of everything and she forgot where she was. The Prowler's hold was too strong. He gripped her mind with a force she could not escape. She was sucked in. He had the ability to make her see the worst version of herself. Panic attached itself. Fears that were deeply hidden became reality and controlled her actions. She must face her darkest thoughts head on.

Alone.

She was taken away to a place she had never known. A place in the recesses of her mind where the Prowler planted false scenarios that she thought really happened. It started with snakes that coiled around her legs and slithered their way up her torso to her face. The snake's slimy scales were cold against her skin. Her stomach churned as bile crept up her throat. She could not think or move. She was paralyzed by the Prowler's hold. He had her right where he wanted her.

The fear became tangible. Soon, the snakes vanished and she was taken to a vivid memory… a real memory. The Regime had invaded her city. It was a month and a half since her parents' deaths. She was back in her prom dress walking with Sky toward Kira when the bomb went off. She was blown off her feet. Warm blood spilled from her chest. Shrapnel found its way through her again, too close to her heart. Her eyes rolled into the back of her head. When she reopened them, she was out of her memory and back into fear.

A man stood before her. His face was blurred out. She tried to make out who he was, but she couldn't. All she knew was the hate she felt toward him.

Do something.

She tried diligently to regain control. She broke free of the hold in her mind and hit the faceless man as hard as she could squarely in the jaw. He vanished and turned to dust that filled the air. The dust stormed through the room she was now enclosed in. She could not breathe. The dust filled her lungs, making her cough until she dry heaved. Fluorescent lights flashed on. They flickered on and off until the electricity shot fully through them. She was boxed in and there was no way out. There were no windows to break through, no doors to unlock. Only fear and silence.

She did her best to break free from the Prowler's hold. She fought with every fiber in her being. She told herself it was just the Prowler's game that played tricks on her mind, but her mind did not believe her. The dust huddled together to form the faceless man again. She still could not make out who he was, but she knew he was her enemy.

He came close to her, his breath hot on her face. His hands snapped around her neck, cutting off her airflow. He shoved her back into the wall. Her feet dangled in the air with his hands still around her neck. She hung like a lifeless rag doll. The only way she could get free from this Prowler was if something inside her fought back harder. Her mind had to grab hold of reality again. It had to believe in something. It needed hope. She said she would be strong, but had never felt so wrong. At this moment, she felt weak—weaker than she'd been her entire life. She had to do something. She searched the depths of her soul and looked for anything that could stand up against him.

Fight. No weapon formed against me shall prosper.

Her faith in Christ was activated and her hope triggered. It radiated through her mind, freeing her body to move once again. She made this man disappear once. She could do it again. She kicked and squirmed until the faceless man lost his grip on her neck. She fell to the ground, grasping for air. The dust vanished.

Clean air filled her lungs. Something wrapped around her waist pulled at her. She was not sure if it was real or if she was still stuck in her head. She heard faint screams behind her, but her sight was still impaired. She could not see her own hands, let alone the person whose voice screamed at her. Another tug pulled at her waist. She was being dragged across the terrain. She was not sure if she should fight it or not. She did not feel afraid anymore.

Her mind cleared and she regained her vision. She saw the rope that was tethered to Sky around her waist.

They had never disconnected it. She let the rope drag her farther from the Prowler's territory as she scrambled to her feet. Sky pulled her closer to him as the Prowler chased after her. He would catch her if she did not run. She spun around and found her feet. She ran fast. Sky had been unaffected by the mind game. The Prowler took Lennox first.

Lennox reached Sky and they ran swiftly over the rocks. The Prowler was closing in on them. They had to keep running until they passed the boundary of his territory so he could not follow them anymore—so they hoped. They dodged barricades and infant trees that stretched out their branches. It wasn't until they passed the three-mile mark from the Prowler's territory that they looked back. He no longer chased them. Sky and Lennox saw the Prowler in the distance. He hissed at them as he retreated.

Lennox threw her head back and sighed in relief. She had almost lost herself. Had she not fought back, she would be a statue, glued to the Prowler's hold the rest of her life. She would also be dead if Sky had not pulled her out when he did.

"How long was I in there?" Lennox asked. It felt like days had passed.

"You were there for almost an hour."

"Really, that's it?" That was long enough. She had her fill of Prowler mind games to last forever. She never wanted to go through that again. The terror that shot through her veins was overwhelming and like nothing else she had ever experienced.

"How did you break free?" Sky asked, out of breath.

"Faith that God was with me. I had to find something stronger on the inside of myself than the Prowler's hold of me." She remembered her brother's words, "Faith is worth fighting for."

"I am glad you broke his hold because I could not pull you out until you did. You were stuck there. I pulled the rope the whole time. It was not until you fell that I could move you," Sky said hunched over, still trying to catch his breath.

"Are we sure he can't come any farther?" Lennox asked, turning back around to see if she could still see the Prowler.

"If he could have, he would have. His eyes were set on keeping you, and if he could not keep you for himself, he would have killed you. I am sure of it. If he could stray far enough from his territory, we both would be dead. Trust me, he can't come any farther," Sky reassured her.

His reassurance would have to be good enough because it was all she was going to get.

Lennox shifted focus when she saw a soldier in black fatigues headed their way. He was alone with a canine that resembled Grizzly. The dog caught their scent and hurdled toward them with its fangs showing. The soldier chased after it. The Prowler's territory blocked their escape. The dog was barely twenty feet away when its master shouted a command, making him halt.

There were not supposed to be any soldiers around here. Lennox suspected they must have veered off course. She was not sure if he saw them yet. Sky and Lennox ran for cover, but the grown trees were too far away. The dog barked incessantly at his master. The soldier stood by the dog's side, walking closer.

"Stop!" they heard the soldier yell. He drew his weapon, ready to fire.

They turned around to meet their fate. The soldier walked closer with the gun still pointed at them. As he approached, his face became clearer. He was a middle-aged man with newly indented lines forming on his tanned skin.

"You should not be here," he said. His face was red with anger, and his teeth were clenched.

"We don't want to be here, but—" Lennox felt Sky's hand on her arm and stopped speaking.

This soldier was dangerous. His eyes were different… vacant. It was strange what fear made people become. Lennox knew that firsthand.

"What am I supposed to do with you two… why aren't you in a city?" The soldier's rage grew with every passing minute in their presence.

Why would they need to be in a city? Did the Regime already take that much control? Lennox prayed, "Lord, give us favor, if even for just a moment."

The soldier's eyes darted back and forth, up and down. He noticed the Sparrow emblem on their suits and shook his head. "I am going to regret this. I know I am, I already do. Run, before I change my mind." He pointed his gun toward the larger pine trees that stood in the distance. He did not look like he would give them another chance.

Sky grabbed Lennox by the arm and whispered, "Run as fast as you can away from him."

They ran and did not look back. The dog barked until they were out of sight. Lennox compared herself to the soldier and contrasted how different their chosen roads were. This war made him almost as inhuman as the

Prowler. The man inside who once had the ability to show compassion was gone. It was a miracle he let them go. That could have been her, or Sky, had they not chosen to leave when they did. After her experience with the Prowler, Lennox never wanted to lose herself again. It was a terrible feeling. When they stopped running, Lennox threw her hands over her head to catch her breath. "I can't believe what some men have become. I wanted to help him realize that he did not have to be a Regime soldier," she said through her breaths.

"No, he had already made up his mind. You could see it in his eyes. He was gone. We were lucky that he even let us go," Sky gasped, stretching out his legs. His face was tired and stressed beyond what Lennox had ever seen before.

"I can't stand to see people lose all hope. It is like they just give up," she sighed, feeling lost and upset at the inhumanity.

"That is why we won't give up." Sky squared his shoulders, making his tall frame even taller and more powerful. "Our hope is not in things of this world. We hope in something greater, always remember that," Sky reminded her. He said it for her as much as he said it for himself.

She must let go of her disappointment and learn that people would disappoint her, one way or the other. She would not let it stop her from her own fight.

The sun was about to wake up from its slumber. They needed to find a place on the map where they could recoup their strength. The mountains had been a setback and the Prowler attack left them exhausted. Their suit's alarms rang in their ears. The only way to silence them was to adhere to their warnings.

"We are only a mile off our original route," Sky said, looking at the map.

They needed to trek that mile to get back on course before they could even consider stopping.

Life grew more abundant. The cedar trees were not as sparse and the ice melted away. Adolescent trees bloomed all around them. The earth was rich and gave life to the small forest. The rubble was gone. This place was uninhabited.

It felt safe to Lennox, so she deactivated her helmet. She could not stand the flashing on the screen or the alarm ringing in her ears. She knew she was tired and hungry. Her stomach growled as a reminder. She did not need the suit to tell her *that*.

When the tech left her face, her five senses were overloaded with the scents and sounds of the place. Her suit had last read the temperature at twenty degrees Fahrenheit, but it felt like the perfect seventy degrees of spring. She raised her eyebrows at Sky. He could not take the alarms either. He turned his helmet off and inhaled the world around him.

"This will work, right?" Lennox was glad to have an easier road to travel for once. Though nothing was easy anymore, and she would take what she could, when she could get it.

"Yeah, it works. Do you hear that?" Sky asked while he leaned his ear closer to the sound. "It sounds like a waterfall."

He was right. They walked a few hundred yards further and saw where all the ice went. It melted in perfect unison into a river surrounded by a meadow. Lennox was thankful the map indicated it was a safe rest stop, or they couldn't stay, no matter how nice it was.

The meadow beckoned Lennox. She sprawled out on the freshly grown grass and listened to the melting ice crash into the river. Sky took off his boots and rolled up the pant legs of his tech suit. He sat on the edge of the bank and stuck his aching feet into the ice-cold water. They could lie down without any barriers in this outdoor sanctuary. It reminded Lennox of God's goodness. She placed her satchel behind her head and let her thoughts drift, forcing herself not to think of the Prowler or the soldier.

The sound of snapping twigs under someone's boots was too close to them. Sky grabbed Lennox by the arm and pulled her up. He shoved his unlaced boots on to his feet. The dog that found them before tracked their scent once again. The soldier who let them go must have changed his mind.

"I knew it was too easy," Sky said through gritted teeth. "Hide!"

The steps came closer.

Lennox's heart pounded in her chest and her body sucked in oxygen noisily. She tried to calm her breathing and hid behind a wide tree trunk. Sky hid behind a tree a few feet away and held a finger to his mouth to signal silence. The dog would sniff them out—no matter how quiet they remained.

She held her breath as the soldier passed by. His body huffed and puffed as he let out unintelligible groans on his radio. Lennox hoped he would give up the hunt. She shifted her weight and a twig snapped. She stiffened against the tree like a statue. The soldier heard the noise and spun in circles, searching. The dog came closer and closer to her tree.

"I know you are out there." The soldier's words broke from short, quick breaths.

Lennox did not move. She held her breath, but the dog sniffed her out and she started to gasp for air. The whole situation seemed unreal. The German shepherd snarled and exposed its teeth, readying itself to lunge at Lennox. Then, the dog froze and stared directly past her. It was as if it looked at something only it could see. Its tail tucked between its legs and it ran away into the woods, whimpering.

The soldier cursed the dog and walked directly to Lennox's tree. Sky catapulted out of his hiding place and knocked the gun out of the soldier's hand. The soldier threw his right fist into Sky's face and it landed squarely on Sky's jaw.

Think, Lennox think! Why can't I think?

She forced her lungs to take in slow, steady breaths.

Oh, God... help us!

She fell to her knees and searched the ground for the

gun. Running her hands through the leaves, the dirt crept up her fingernails. Her right hand hit the metal barrel as she fumbled over it. Picking up the gun, her hands shook out of her control. Her finger rested on the trigger as she took aim at the soldier's back. She could not pull the trigger. She had just finished senior year. She was not a soldier, not a fighter.

Yet, here she was.

Sky and the soldier fell to the ground, intertwined in battle. Their bodies rolled over one another and the leaves rustled around them.

God help me!

Lennox walked closer to the brawl and raised the gun over her head, intending to bring it down with as much force as she could. It hit the soldier on the back of the head and his body went limp. With tears of fear running down her cheeks, the gun fell from her hand back into the leaves where she found it. Adrenaline pumped through her as she reached for Sky. His swollen jaw dropped as he took a deep breath and rolled the soldier off.

"I—I didn't know what else to do," Lennox said, sucking in the air with short and quick gasps.

"You did good, it's okay. They're going to send more

soldiers to find him, so we have to get out of here, now."

"You're hurt," Lennox said, looking at Sky's face. His lip was swollen, and his nose bled. She could not understand how he was so calm, but she was glad he was... because she was not.

"I'm fine. We have to get out of here."

Their feet flew over the crisp leaves and pushed them through the woods. Branches hit their faces as they passed by.

Chapter 18

The meadow and trees gave way to another ice land. Night fell, causing the temperature to drop well below zero. Lennox longed for the warmth of the meadow. How did the Regime change the atmosphere like they had? With that kind of machine, they could change the world for the better instead of using it as a weapon of mass destruction. But the Regime wanted war, not peace. The weapon was for control, not unity.

The sky was full of stars, which made it feel a little less dark and a little less cold to Lennox. The silver moon peeked through the one lonely cloud in the night. A thick layer of ice made it hard to run fast—or run at all—for that matter. They could glide from one place to another if it weren't for the rubble that hindered their path.

Sky and Lennox could go no farther. They made the decision to rest at the next checkpoint. Their bodies grew weaker and their minds were tested every minute with every noise they heard. They had no idea how close the soldier could be to finding them again, even though Lennox knocked him out. He would bring reinforcements, but their bodies demanded pause.

"We should search for food," Sky said, holding his stomach.

"Okay, I'll go look over there if you want to look in the other direction." Lennox was reminded of her own hunger.

She gathered whatever berries she found as she picked through the ruins of a city. Nearly everything was frozen over. It would take a miracle for them to find any sustenance. When Lennox bent over one last frost-covered bush, a flash of silver sped right in front of her. It stopped and she saw a figure stand by a disintegrated building.

"Who are you?" she asked with a shakier voice than she intended. She wanted to yell for Sky, but knew it was no use because this person was already too close for Sky to be of assistance.

She looked beyond the clear guard of the helmet and saw a face that was worn and tired—like her own. Picking up a piece of metal, Lennox held it like a baseball bat, ready to hit the boy who appeared to be barely older than she was. The light from his suit lit up his olive skin. His hair was so black that it was almost blue. His eyes were dark brown with flecks of gold.

He raised his hands in surrender. "I am not the Regime! I am not the Regime! I'm just someone who got separated from their group." He tugged at his sleeve and Lennox saw the same Sparrow emblem on his suit.

The familiar outline of the bird made her give a heavy sigh as she rested the metal on top of her shoulder— unwilling to set it down just yet. She surprised herself with her audacity to fight if necessary.

"My name is Ander," he explained. "I got lost when fog covered the land my group was in. I think I'm going in circles. You are the first person I've seen since."

Lennox pointed Ander in the direction where Sky made camp. Ander walked through first. Sky was on one knee. He stood to his feet and his eyes grew wide as Ander walked closer with Lennox close behind, the metal bar still in her hands. Ander stretched out his right hand toward Sky.

"Hi, I'm Ander."

Sky shook his hand, and his eyes shifted to Lennox.

"He got lost from his group," she said.

"How?" Sky stared straight through Ander.

"Fog. I could not see a foot in front of me, let alone where my group was," Ander explained.

"How big was your group?" Lennox asked.

"There were four of us. We had been on the run for months trying to find safety. We ran into a few Sparrows who gave us these suits," he said, pinching the fabric of the all-terrain suit. "They told us about some kind of city of refuge called Sparrow City, but we kept getting lost and turned around when the weather changed." Ander stopped talking and rubbed the back of his neck.

"We are headed for Sparrow City too and have a map. You can travel with us," Sky said.

Lennox knew he was just as sympathetic of Ander's trials as she was, but she balked at his willingness to include Ander in the rest of their journey. They had to help him, she knew that, but Sky's willingness surprised her. It was what her parents and Sky's pop would have done.

"Thank you," Ander smiled at Sky and nodded to Lennox. "I mean it, thank you," he said again, clutching his right hand to his left shoulder.

He seemed a little awkward when meeting new people, just as Lennox knew she would be if she were in the same situation.

"We were just about to stop and rest for the night," Lennox informed him as she sat down on a piece of cement.

"Rest sounds good."

Lennox saw Ander's eyes were more bloodshot than she noticed before. They were also dark with puffy circles underneath.

"Y'all go to sleep. I will keep watch."

Sky took the metal bar that Lennox rested against her knee. She looked up at him and shrugged her shoulders.

Lennox folded her body onto the cement rubble and slept. Nightmares assaulted her rest again. Her parents, Kira, and Oliver formed knots in her stomach as sweat gathered on her forehead, even with the suit on. Her eyes flew open as she shot up from her labored sleep.

When she looked around, she noticed Sky was asleep and Ander had taken over the watch. She sat up and smiled, surprised Sky trusted Ander enough to sleep. He must have made Sky comfortable enough in the short time they had talked.

Ander gave Lennox a slight wave as he sipped water from a canteen. He cleared his throat and screwed the lid back on. "Nightmares? I get them too."

Lennox shifted her weight on the cement and crossed

her legs, "Yeah, they're the worst. I keep seeing my parents and everyone else I had to leave behind."

Ander sat straighter, "Mine are the same every time. I see my parents one minute and then the next, the floodwaters sweep them away. I reach out for them, but it is too late." He put his hands on his temples and looked down. "Apparently, Ahab did not like that my city refused to give up Bibles at the mass book burning."

Give up Bibles? Was it already that extreme? The burning of Bibles reminded her of Pop's words about the birth of the American Underground Church. She never thought there would be a need for such a thing. Lennox's heart hurt for Ander and she forced a painful smile. He knew the exact pain she did.

"I'm so sorry," she said, glad to see Ander open up a little bit about what he had been through, however tragic it was.

"Yeah, the Regime has stolen everything from me, and it haunts me." Ander took a deep breath and stood up to stretch out his legs.

"Do you still trust God?" Lennox asked, wanting to give him hope. She knew that being on the run after losing everything made it hard to believe, and even harder to trust. It was a constant struggle to have faith.

One minute, life was normal, and in the next, normalcy was stripped away. If his city was controlled to the point where the Regime burned Bibles, she was sure her city was too. She had to trust God even more.

"I want to," he said, sitting back down.

"Me too." Lennox gave another pained smile. She wanted him to know that he was not alone but did not know exactly what to say.

Lennox turned from Ander for a moment and noticed Sky's sketchbook was out. It distracted her from their conversation. Sky never left it lying out. He always tucked it away, deep in his pack. She knew how private he was about his drawings, and she remembered him at school when he said he was not very good and was embarrassed to show anyone. He said he drew because he enjoyed it. It helped him cope the same way writing helped Lennox. It kept his mind occupied so thoughts of war and leaving Pop behind would not overtake him. He must have been so tired after his watch that he forgot to put it up.

Lennox picked the sketchbook up off the ground with the intention of putting it up for him when a loose sketch fell out from the hundreds of other pages. It was a sketch of a girl that looked a whole lot like her. Ander looked at Lennox and smiled again. She nervously smiled back without saying a word. She did not want to draw attention to the sketch she held in her hands. Sky would not want her to see it.

Lennox was in disbelief at her portrayal. The sketched girl's features were delicate and feminine. She had a heart shaped face with almond shaped eyes and long lashes. There was an aura of bravery about her with fierceness in her eyes. This wasn't how Lennox saw herself, but it was how Sky saw her.

Lennox felt her feelings for Sky grow stronger. She couldn't stop them if she wanted to. She blushed and hoped he knew how much his view of her mattered. The question—whether or not he still saw her as just his best friend—was answered by the sketch. She saw how he observed the real Lennox by the details and time he invested in the drawing. He viewed her much as she viewed him—with respect and admiration.

Lennox tucked the loose page back into the book and secured it in the folds of the other pages. She buried the sketchbook deep into Sky's pack. She hoped that Ander would not bring it up. Why would he? He did not know what it was.

Sky stirred and stretched out his long limbs. "We

should get moving," he said with a yawn.

"Yeah, we should, but we should eat first. Do you have food?" Ander asked.

"All I could find were berries," Lennox said, pointing to where she put them.

Their stomachs forgot for a brief moment how hungry they were.

"I hate to say this, but we are going to have to raid a city. It's our only choice. Maybe I can get the soldier MREs that don't have trackers." Sky only looked to Lennox for approval.

She loathed the idea of raiding a city, but they had no other choice. The distance they walked daily, required massive calorie intake that they were not getting. They would pass out before long. Water could only sustain them for a short time.

"There is a Regime stronghold not too far from here," Ander said.

"Lennox, give him the map so he can show us where it is."

Lennox did not want to go near the Regime, but she knew they needed the food to provide the necessary energy to deliver the locket to Sparrow City. So she handed the map to Ander, and he led the way.

They traveled miles to a city that was left in ruins like the desert city and ice land—only it was much worse. It looked like a tornado rummaged through it and a lightning storm incinerated it. The charred debris gave way to blackened ice. Lennox thought of Ander's parents and put her hand on her neck where the locket hid behind her suit.

It can change everything.

Their conversation turned silent. There was nothing to be said.

Scorched buildings crumpled on the still, frozen landscape. Vehicles were torn in half with their pieces yards apart. An abandoned airport was demolished, its planes iced over in their hangers. Makeshift graves eerily lined the walkway with crosses on the left and right. It was hallowed ground. The survivors must have buried those who died before they fled or perished themselves in a different storm. Lennox hoped that many escaped.

She was thankful that their trek would soon be over. One day, they would eventually make it to Sparrow City. One day, they would be safe again. They would not have to run anymore. One day, they could even make a difference. Lennox wanted that "one day" to come... soon.

Chapter 19

The map did not tell them that the next city they passed would be a Regime industrial city. Orange lights lit up a Regime building, marking every point of its tall industrial towers. The lights aligned like constellations in the night sky and smoke billowed up into the atmosphere from the highest points on the towers.

"We need to stake out the city and figure out the best way in," Sky said, walking slowly.

The trees towered hundreds of feet high with their leaves spread thick. They were the perfect cover for spying.

The city was a fortress. Lennox knew it was one of the worst cities to raid. It appeared to be where the Regime's weapons were made. Only workers and their families were visible and they all wore the same standard tan jumpsuit—even the children. They would need to steal clothes to blend in.

Sneaking in looked hard, too. Electric fences fully encompassed the city. The only way in was if they were covert enough to hitch a ride on one of the work trucks that were permitted on and off the city grounds to bring in supplies.

They deactivated their helmets, which read seventy-five degrees Fahrenheit. They figured the GWS was not used near Regime strongholds. It was the first, in what felt like a long time, that they could take off their entire suits. They took them off and stuffed them in their packs. Lennox stared at her boots, realizing that they were the only ones she had.

"What about our boots? If anyone notices them they will know we are outsiders." Lennox pulled her pant legs down as far as she could.

"We will get some other boots when we get our jumpsuits."

Sky had no way of knowing how easy they would be to get, but Lennox chose to trust that God would provide what they needed. He was their only hope.

Lennox's t-shirt and jeans were smudged with dirt. She looked over at Sky. So were his. Ander wore a black t-shirt and tan cargo pants that were cleaner than theirs, but still dirty. She worried they would stand out too much before they got the new jumpsuits. She shook the feelings of worry and walked over to where Sky and Ander crouched down, looking at the road and waiting to see the trucks. She tucked the locket safely behind her shirt and took a deep breath.

"We walk by faith, not by sight," she thought.

It did not matter what it looked like. They would get through. She had to believe they would make it to Sparrow City.

They had to.

They watched as a line of trucks pulled from behind the electric fence to pick up supplies. They would wait until the caravan came back before they would sneak on one to get in the city.

Time was not on their side. It took too long for the trucks to get back and it was already 5 a.m. According to Eli's information, that meant they only had two hours to get in and out before the anthem played at 7 a.m. They needed three hours, at least. This city was too big to raid in only two.

The trucks returned and stopped at a checkpoint heavily saturated with guards. The road was narrow and bordered by a thick line of trees. The same trees they hid behind at the stakeout were the same ones that would allow them to sneak on a truck. Guards randomly selected trucks to search for intruders, so they must choose one without second-guessing their choice while the soldiers searched another.

Sky chose one with an olive-green canvas canopy that covered the back. It was the second to last vehicle in line and was full of blankets and medical supplies for the hospital. The industrial cities had larger hospitals due to a high ratio of accidents. This truck was their best option. They made a break for it and climbed quietly into the truck bed. They laid down flat, putting the blankets and medical supplies in front of and on top of them. They all lay as still as possible when they felt the truck move.

They made it!

Their bodies swayed into each other with the jerky movement of alternating gas and brake. The truck rolled to a stop a few feet from where they jumped in. Ander looked at Sky and then at Lennox.

The truck in front of them was selected for a search. That was good news and bad news. It meant the chances of their truck being searched were slim, but it also meant soldiers were all around them. Lennox's heart pounded in her chest like when the soldier chased after them in the woods. If the guards sensed something was amiss, they would get caught.

Lennox heard a soldier directly outside the back of the truck and covered her mouth with her hands to mask her frantic breathing.

"Get the K9 unit out here!" the soldier shouted at the top of his lungs.

The K9 unit would sniff them out just like the dog in the woods. Lennox was sure of it. Sky looked at an antsy Ander and shook his head "No". He could tell what Ander was thinking. Ander looked like he wanted to bolt.

The wind caught the truck's canvas and it flapped against the metal side noisily. The sudden sound startled them. The truck rolled forward again and this time it did not stop. Lennox uncovered her mouth and let out a sigh of relief. The K9 unit went right past them without a second look. The dogs sniffed out a trail that led away from their occupied truck. The soldiers must be searching for someone, or something else. The dogs ran beside their masters all the way into the woods, opposite of where Sky, Lennox, and Ander came from.

The truck slowed, then parked. Lennox peered

through the gaps in the canvas. They were in a hospital garage. The passenger's side door creaked open and closed, and then the driver's side door opened and slammed shut. Two industrial men walked to the back of the truck by the tailgate. Lennox, Sky, and Ander froze. The men carried on a conversation for a few minutes before they left, leaving the supplies and inhabitants in the truck. Sky quietly moved all the supplies back in order and crawled out.

"That was too close," Lennox whispered as Sky helped her down.

Ander jumped out after her. Sweat rolled down his face and neck.

"It was not too close. It's only *too* close if you get caught," Sky countered.

He was right. Their lives were made up of close calls now.

Sky rummaged through the back of several trucks. There were no jumpsuits to steal in the garage. They had to look for them somewhere else. It would not be easy. Their jeans and t-shirts were a dead giveaway they did not belong there.

The service elevator dinged. They had to hide!

Sky ran to the front of the truck as Lennox and Ander

followed behind. They crouched down by the headlights of the truck they were just in. Ander flinched from the heat of the engine. He rested his hand on the hood.

"Ouch!"

"Shhh!" Sky and Lennox turned to him simultaneously with their pointer fingers pressed to their lips.

Ander lowered his head and mouthed the word "Sorry."

They waited impatiently and watched to see who would emerge from the elevator. The door opened with no one inside. Lennox and Sky looked at each other and shrugged their shoulders questioningly. It was eerie the way the elevator's door slid shut.

"Come on, let's go," Sky urged and led the way.

"Where are we going? Are we going to use the elevator? There are cameras in there," Ander said worriedly.

"No, we are going to use the stairwell right across from the elevator," Sky reassured.

The door was just unlocked with an access key and was closing. Sky grabbed Lennox's hand and ran to the door. Ander followed on their heels. Sky could leave them behind and run faster if he wanted to, but instead he made sure he went no faster than they could. Sky slid his hand in between the door and the lock just before it had time to click shut. They waited until they no longer heard footsteps on the stairs, and then started to climb.

The stairwell went up three stories. They checked the first floor. It was riddled with patients and doctors. The second floor held patient's rooms. The third floor contained offices and storage. It would have the jumpsuits they needed.

Sky poked his head around the third-floor door. It was all clear. He signaled Lennox and Ander through the door and into the hall. The doctors were in their offices with their heads down, busied by paperwork and oblivious to their intruders' presence.

Lennox checked the doors to empty offices as Sky and Ander kept watch, but they were locked. Lennox shook her head as she moved on to the next door. She surveyed one last door that was windowless. It was risky, but she turned the stainless steel handle and it opened.

They cut by the door and the smell of bleach burned their noses. It was a nurses' closet with blankets, medical supplies, jumpsuits, and boots. There were a dozen tan suits freshly laundered and neatly folded on a shelf with boots lined up beside them. Sky grabbed a size large and threw Lennox a small. Ander snatched a large and put it on over his clothes. With their tan Regime jumpsuits and boots, they were free to walk the main level of the hospital and around the city, but they needed to sneak off the current floor first. Only doctors and nurses were allowed on the third floor.

Lennox opened the closet door, peeked her head through, and looked around. A doctor left his office. She shut the door quickly, keeping the knob turned so it would not make a noise. She cracked it open again and saw the doctor disappear into the elevator. They walked from the closet back to the stairwell, acting like they were meant to be there and making sure they did not draw attention to themselves. They flew down the stairs to the first floor and matched their pace to the industrial workers.

First aid kits and MREs were their top priorities. They brushed the first aid kits that sat on the emergency room's counters into their bags. They never knew when they would need them again.

They passed through some sliding doors and noticed a soldier's station a few feet in front of them. A cafeteria was located about fifty feet to the right of it. Its food would not have trackers like everyone else's. Soldiers left the city frequently and it seemed pointless to place trackers in their food. At least, that's what Lennox thought.

"Lennox, you and Ander go and wait for me in the cafeteria," Sky said, pointing to the large rectangle building.

"Where are you going?" Lennox asked, scrunching her eyebrows together. She hated when he left her. It meant he was about to do something dangerous and he did not want her to get hurt.

"I'm going to get MREs out of the soldier bunker over there." He pointed to the soldier's station.

Lennox watched as Sky sauntered over to the station. She and Ander watched him walk away slow and steady with his head held low. Very few people paid Sky any attention. A few gave second glances, but then returned to what occupied them. Lennox sat with Ander in the cafeteria. A clock read 6:30 a.m. They had thirty minutes left to get out of the city. Lennox tapped her foot hoping to see Sky walk back any minute. She rested her hand on top of the locket.

"Hurry up, Sky," she mumbled under her breath.

"Um, Lennox? We can't stay here," Ander said,

rubbing his temples with his palms as his elbows rested on the table.

He stood up to leave and Lennox casually followed him. They walked through a cluster of workers with their heads down. The building was aligned with an electric fence. They saw it from the cafeteria's windows. They went outside and checked for a weak spot or opening they could squeeze through.

There was none.

The electricity that coursed through the links of the fence was inescapable. Warning signs for high voltage were liberally plastered on the fence, and razor wire formed circular patterns on the top. Even if they wanted to cut through or climb over, they couldn't. Lennox wouldn't leave Sky anyway. Sky would come back for her, and she would be there when he did. There was no way she would leave him in the city alone.

Lennox's mind raced, making her body pace back and forth. Ander laced his fingers together and rested them on top of his head. He walked back to the front of the building. He was flustered with their lack of options. So was Lennox.

"Maybe we can make it out to the trucks or hide somewhere." She was hopeful there would be another way out when they found Sky.

"I don't think we will make it to the trucks… and there's nowhere to hide." Ander reviewed the situation in his head.

"So, what do you suggest?" she asked, frustrated. She thought hiding was their best bet.

"We are going to have to go out in the open with everyone else."

"And do what? Bow?" Lennox was shocked and revolted at the idea.

Time dwindled away.

"We should have been smarter with our timing. We should have waited in the woods until after the anthem played. We were stupid to have come in here when we did."

Ander walked out from behind the cafeteria building and into the open. Lennox followed after him. The minutes ticked away.

Two minutes left… one minute left… thirty seconds…

That was all the time they had. The 7 a.m. anthem played over the intercom. One by one, people filed out to the city streets. There was an ocean of tan jumpsuits. Men, women, and children stopped what they were doing and bowed, all facing the same direction. Lennox thought of the video she saw at the cabin. They were driven like moths to a flame. Whether out of fear or respect for Ahab, they all bowed.

A red ball that children had been playing foursquare with bounced down the street. No one acknowledged it. No one stopped it from bouncing away. Lennox wanted to be that red ball, invisible to the people bowing and the Regime that stood guard.

Chapter 20

Lennox wasn't invisible. There was nowhere to escape… nowhere to run. They stood out in the open while the anthem rang loud and clear. It sounded like a bass drum echoing in the air. Emotions flooded her senses. She did not know how to respond. It was only a matter of seconds before someone confronted them for standing. They had to make a choice.

Lennox turned to look back at the Regime soldiers. They herded a few of the stragglers together, mainly older workers. She glanced to the soldier's station where Sky was supposed to be and saw nothing but more soldiers. Sky was nowhere to be seen. Her heart dropped. She felt hopeless.

When she turned back around, Ander was gone. Her heart sank further. She twisted her body around to see if she could see him anywhere. She saw nothing. No places to hide, no places that she had missed to run to.

Where could he have gone?

He would have never left her. Then again—she didn't know him very well. Maybe he would have. Maybe he had.

She searched again for Sky and looked in the direction she was certain he should be, but did not find him. He was gone, too. Thoughts of Sky raced through her mind. It did not make sense. He would not leave her behind.

Sky, where are you?

The stragglers were rounded up. This was her last chance to make a choice, or it would be made for her. Her eyes roamed one last time in a last attempt to find them. They rested on Ander... a face in the crowd... bowing.

Lennox's eyes must have deceived her. Ander would never bow to a man who destroyed his city and stole his parents. Sky would never leave her out in the open alone, either. She knew this had to be a bad dream, a nightmare. She closed her eyes, but it changed nothing. When she opened them, everything was just as it was before. She was the only one left standing in defiance. She was alone. She felt a thousand people looking at her, but she only cared about two.

Sky and Ander. She fixed her eyes on Ander. He refused to look at her.

Coward.

They had only just met, but she never guessed he was one to betray his faith. She was wrong.

A storm of confusion that mixed with anger swirled in her head. A voice broke her stare.

"Bow!"

It was a command.

She thought of the woman's body that she saw dragged away into the darkness on the screen. Her heart raced. Her flesh cautioned her to bow and step back from the line of fire, but her faith would not let her. She could not stop herself from crying. A tear fell down her cheek and rolled down her neck.

The voice repeated itself. "Bow, I said!"

When she had nothing left to lose, she found out who she really was. She felt the girl she always wanted to be rise up inside her. She screamed for Lennox to set her free, begged for her to be brave.

Lennox took a deep breath. She had come a long way from that fearful girl she used to be. She had been through too much to give in now. Her faith unfurled like an eagle's wings on their first flight. Courage found her.

With gritted teeth and clenched fists, she managed to say, "No." Her throat was tight, but her voice was powerful.

She blinked away the tears that blurred her vision of Ander and looked up to the heavens. She exhaled. She made her choice all on her own. Not for Ander... not for Sky... not for Oliver... but for herself. She could only choose for herself. It was the most difficult thing she had ever done. Nothing compared to this moment. She was so vulnerable, yet she never felt stronger. Something sparked within, and she remembered—in her weakness God was made strong. She was more alive than she had ever been. She felt a lion roar deep inside. Her faith in God was worth fighting for, worth standing for. Only *He* was her salvation. Only *He* was her God. She bowed only to Him.

The voice that yelled the command came into view. He was a terribly large man with a buzz cut and enormous forehead. He bore a scar that ran over his left eye that made his face frozen with a permanent scowl. He was not happy with her. His huge fists were curled into balls that looked like hammers. His fists alone looked like they could cause a whole lot of damage. He charged closer. He smelled of tobacco as he breathed the words into Lennox's face.

"What did you say?"

Lennox squared her shoulders and stood tall. Faith fused her bones together and shut out fear. Doubt was closed off and fear became a part of her past with no part in her present. She would not be intimidated. She would not be afraid. It did not matter the consequence.

She would *fight*.

"I said, no!" She spoke clearer this time and with confidence. There was no denying what she had just said.

She heard gasps in the crowd. The last time they saw someone stand during the anthem was probably months ago. If you wanted to eat, you bowed. If you wanted to live, you bowed.

An old woman nearby with a face full of wrinkles tugged on Lennox's pant leg. "Bow, you stupid girl!"

Lennox ignored her. She focused her heart and mind on her parents, knowing they would be proud of her decision to stand.

The locket!

Lennox made sure her tan Regime jumpsuit still rested on top of the locket, hiding it safely away from the soldier's view.

The unhappy man kicked away the old woman's hand

and pulled out his metal baton. Lennox felt the full weight of it smash against the back of her knees. She fell to her hands. A foot met her back and pushed her down flat. A strong palm crushed her face into the dirt. Her lip busted open and she tasted blood. Her eyes found the coward—Ander. He looked right through her. His face was expressionless. She was a stranger to him, and he was a stranger to her.

"You are under arrest for being a Defier of the Regime. You will be punished according to your crime," the man said.

Lennox's hands were zip-tied together behind her back and she was jerked to her feet. They pushed her away from the crowd. Faces gazed at her in horror. Some laughed, but most shook their heads at the stupid girl who stood for her faith in Christ. They knew that it could be them too if they dared defy the Regime, but they did not see it as a good enough reason to be labeled a Defier. However, Lennox knew her eternity was at stake. She would not throw away her confidence in Christ so easily.

Lennox did everything she could not to look back at Ander. She could not bear to see his face anymore.

Where is Sky?

Her thoughts traveled to distant memories of her and

Sky. She could not understand how he left her behind without a fight. Maybe he was captured too... or worse... maybe he bowed, like Ander.

The Regime soldiers were brutal, but she did not hate them for it. They were pawns on a chessboard. They were puppets to the Regime. Their cruelty was a representation of what they were commanded to do. They feared standing up against the unjust acts of the Regime and Ahab. Fear made them do unspeakable things. Fear made them cowards. It turned them into persons they never wanted to be. Lennox forgave them for their fear because she had once known it all too well herself.

She was blindfolded and thrown into the back of a truck. The driver sped off, causing her to lose her balance. She almost fell off the edge of the truck bed. An exposed piece of metal sliced her arm when she tried to keep herself from falling. It stung.

She was thankful the drive was short. The driver slammed on the brakes, causing her to fly forward. Her body clunked against the metal surface. The driver door swung open and loud feet stomped to the back of the truck. The tailgate opened with a thump.

"Out!"

A one-worded order that Lennox could obey.

She crept her way toward the open tailgate, unsure of where it ended. As she scooted closer to the edge, a hand harshly pulled her out. She fell out of the truck but landed on her feet, which gave her a little satisfaction. She heard someone fumble with keys to unlock a gate. Something that sounded like a chain link fence opened.

She was being thrown into prison. There was no need for a trial. There were no trials anymore. She was found guilty of being a Defier, which was true. Even if she had a trial, she would be found guilty of standing against the Regime.

Chapter 21

The blindfold was abruptly torn from Lennox's face. Red dirt saturated the earth. It crunched under her boots as she shifted her weight. A teenage boy in black fatigues with a hooked nose took a small knife out of his pocket. He could not be much older than Lennox. He came straight toward her with hate in his glare.

She should be frightened, but she wasn't. This boy did not scare her. She figured nothing else would anymore. She learned she was only responsible for how she responded to his hate. Their anger and hate would not define her. It would not shape her, and it would not break her. She had found her strength and her voice. Her hope was in something far greater. Her hope was in Jesus. She gave up roller coaster faith and clung to the promise God gave her. This earth was temporal. What she strived for was eternal.

"My name is Thompson," the boy said with a voice

deeper than Lennox expected.

He was much taller when he stood right next to her. From a distance, he did not look that big. Lennox remained unshaken and said nothing. There was no need to reply. He knew who she was and he knew why she was there. She was a Defier and must be punished. Her world did not align with this new world Commander Ahab created. She was an outcast, and she was okay with that.

Thompson spun her around and cut the zip tie that bound her hands and led her by the arm a few feet. All Lennox could do was walk and stare at the ground.

"So you're the girl who stood, huh? You're pretty stupid, aren't you?" Thompson spat in disgust. "All you had to do was bow."

Lennox did not answer. It made his face turn a violent red. He jerked her to a stop in front of a thick metal door. He threw her in a five-by-six isolation box made for disruptive prisoners. The door slammed shut. The rusted hinges scraped together, sounding like squealing pigs before slaughter. The padlock clicked into place and Lennox was left alone.

The box had no windows for light to break through. Her pupils adjusted to the darkness and the smell of filth assaulted her nostrils. She resolved to not let solitary confinement hinder her. She could not turn back to who she used to be. She made doubt flee from her thoughts. Solitude gave her time to think and pray. She held the locket and willed herself to have faith. She knew isolation had the power to break her, but she chose to let it strengthen her. She discovered that, though her body was in prison, her spirit was free. She quoted the "Lord's Prayer" to ease any fear that tried to rise.

"Our Father, who art in Heaven hallowed be thy name, thy kingdom come, thy will be done on earth as it is in Heaven. Give us this day our daily bread and forgive us our debts as we also have forgiven our debtors, and lead us not into temptation but deliver us from evil...."

God would deliver her from this evil, but even if He didn't, He was still God and He was still good. She reminded herself that no matter how much she wanted to hate Thompson and the Regime, she had to forgive, just as Christ forgave her. She put her faith in God and she knew He would not fail her. She had to learn not to fail Him.

Lennox remained in the box for days. She breathed all the oxygen in the stale air. Her lips were cracked, and her throat yearned for just a drop of water. She crouched down the wall and bent her knees to her chest, wrapping her arms around them. She rested her head on her knees. The 7 p.m. anthem passed… then the 7 a.m.…. then the 7 p.m. again.

She did not know if they would ever let her out. She would not eat or drink that day… or the next. They could deteriorate her body, but she would not let them touch her soul. She reminded herself that God was her strength. This was trusting Him with the "even if He doesn't" kind of faith the Hebrew boys had. They didn't give in and neither would she.

Her flesh was dehydrated and weak when Thompson finally decided to open the door again.

"Rise and shine, sleeping beauty." Lennox was sure this was not a term of endearment . "It is time to get up and work," he said.

Her body struggled to stand. She was dizzy from the light her eyes were denied of for days. She squinted to see Thompson holding open the door—his metal baton was in his other hand. He used it to point to a ditch.

"Start helping the others dig."

The sun rose above the industrial city. The prison camp looked to be a few miles away. Lennox still wondered if Sky was there.

Did he bow too?

She walked to the ditch and peered inside. There were already about fifty prisoners that dug. The youngest prisoner looked no older than twelve. The majority of prisoners seemed like they had civilian backgrounds, and a few looked like Sparrows. They all shared the encircled *D* on the inside of their left forearm under their rolled sleeves.

Lennox slid her body down into the ditch and grabbed the nearest shovel. Thompson and several other guards had their guns slung over their shoulders and their batons in hand. They were ready for battle should any prisoner decide to use the shovel as a weapon. There were twice as many prisoners as there were guards. The prisoners could takeover if they planned it right. Lennox's thoughts filled with ideas of how to escape with her fellow inmates.

A chain link fence that coursed with electricity surrounded the campground just like in the city. They were all prisoners, both soldiers and Defiers. It didn't matter which fence held them in.

Heaps of dirt were thrown to the top of the ditch. Lennox's body struggled to contribute to the pile. The dirt was too hard and her muscles lacked the fortitude to break it up. The morbid thought they dug their own graves entered into her mind, but she shook it away as fast as it came. She could not afford to think like that.

The guards conversed with each other and got caught up in themselves. The youngest prisoner took notice of their lack of attention and crept closer. She was smart. She could sense when one of the guards glanced down, and she dug her shovel to the ground and acted like she worked until they looked away. At first, Lennox thought she was a little boy because she wore a hat with her blonde hair tucked underneath it. The prisoner jumpsuit they gave her was twice her size. The sleeves hung over her hands, and the pant legs were rolled up, but still covered her shoes. Its tan color was made dark with the dirt she shoveled. Dirt was smudged all over her face. Her blue eyes stared right through Lennox.

"Hi, I'm Clover," she whispered. One could still hear the youth in her voice. "Drink as much you want."

She handed Lennox her canteen—she could only refill it when they allowed her to. She also gave Lennox a dirty slice of bread that she had hidden away in her sock. Lennox did not complain. She was hungry enough to eat almost anything. The bread and water gave Lennox a boost of energy and took away her dizziness.

"Thank you for the food and water. My name's Lennox," she whispered back to Clover.

"I know who you are. I heard your story going around the prison camp," she whispered.

"You did?" Lennox said surprised. She wiped the sweat from her brow and tried to ignore her body's fatigue. She could not give in to the lightheaded feeling and pass out. She concentrated on the little girl's face.

"Yeah, you're the girl who stood. The guards call you foolish, but I think you are really brave." Clover looked at Lennox like she saw a hero.

Lennox gave a slightly uncomfortable laugh. "Thanks."

Clover must have been brave too. Lennox wanted to know why she was a prisoner, but it would have to wait.

The guards stiffened to a salute as a well-dressed man passed by. He did not fit the appearance of a prison resident or member of the industrial city. He was neither clothed in a tan jumpsuit nor in black fatigues. Instead, he wore a suit that looked tailor-made for him. He nodded at the guards, freeing them from their stance. He headed toward an office that was out of Lennox's view.

Clover went back to digging. She was so intent on making the biggest pile of dirt it was as if she competed to see who could shovel the most. Soon, her dirt piled high above the rest. Lennox wanted to know her even more. She was a sight to see. This little girl was amazing.

Lennox heaved the dirt up into a pile as best as she could. The dirt found its way under her nails and blisters formed on her hands.

A loud whistle sounded. The prisoners dropped their shovels in the ditch and formed a line to help one another climb out. A middle-aged man with weathered skin reached his mud caked hand down to Clover, and then to Lennox, who grabbed hold to climb out. Thompson saw the man helping and kicked him in the back, making him fall head first into the ditch. Lennox's back slammed into the ground and caused the oxygen to leave her lungs. She gasped while she held her chest. The man who helped her was back on his feet, dusting himself off.

"That's not the first time that has happened." He smiled and stretched his back.

She was not sure how he smiled when he must be hurt.

Thompson towered over them. His nose was all Lennox saw.

"No talking! Get out of the ditch and get in line." Thompson narrowed his eyes with a tight face.

"Thompson!" a shout from the office called. With that, the teenage soldier was gone.

"Thanks for helping me. I am sorry about getting you in trouble," Lennox said to the man.

"It is not your fault. Thompson has never liked me."

"Does he like anyone?" she retorted.

The man laughed and shook his head. He gave Lennox his knee to use as a step to climb out of the steep ditch. She turned around to lend him a hand once she was up, but he already pulled himself out. He ran to the single file line before she caught his name. She followed his lead.

No one talked. Everyone was on their best behavior. Lennox learned it was lunchtime, and if you got into any trouble, you lost half of your already menial portion. No one could afford to lose any food.

Entering the prison lunchroom was daunting. Fellow prisoners slopped the meal onto plates. The food looked like it used to be meatloaf and a roll. Prisoners were allowed the leftovers from the industrial workers' plates.

Lennox took her portion to the nearest table. She did not want to sit with anyone and get them in trouble. She took the first bite, knowing she filled her body with trackers, but she had no other choice. Her stomach demanded nutrients. Clover joined her, bumping Lennox's shoulder as she sat down. Lennox figured Clover did not care about the trouble she could get in to by sitting next to her.

"Hey," Clover said casually as if at school lunch.

"Hey," Lennox replied with a mouth full of bread.

"You know the man who helped you has been here the longest," she said.

"No, I didn't know that. What is his name?" Lennox asked, thinking he would make a good Sparrow.

"His name is Ryker. He was a preacher. He has been here since the fallout."

"The fallout?"

"Yeah, when the Regime took over everywhere."

Everyone had different terms for what happened around them, but they all had the same meaning. The Regime infiltrated one of the last freestanding nations. It would not be long until they controlled the entire world.

"So how did you get here?" Lennox asked Clover as she ate.

Clover's face fell and her countenance changed.

"You don't have to tell me if you don't want to."

Lennox felt bad for asking. Of course, it would not be an easy story to tell. No one had easy stories anymore.

"No, I want to." Clover put her fork down and stared into the distance for a moment.

Lennox knew that painful memories would stir up when Clover told her story, so she remained quiet and listened compassionately to every word Clover spoke. With her face growing red and tears swelling in her eyes, Clover started to talk.

"My parents were taken away a few months ago. I got to stay with my brother who is older, but when the Regime raided our house, they found my mother's journal hidden under my mattress. It had Bible verses in it. Instead of protecting me, my brother surrendered and gave me up. They took me, and I have been in here ever since."

Lennox could not imagine her own brother giving her up. Oliver would never do that to her. He always protected her, and she couldn't understand how anyone could betray their own family like that. What kind of vile person gives up a twelve-year-old little girl?

Clover wiped the tears away and added one last fact. "My brother is Thompson."

Lennox's face fell. She did not know what to say. She

looked at Thompson who stood outside the door. She wanted to hit something… hit him… but knew that would help nothing. She wished Sky were here. He would know what to say. There was nothing she could say or do that would make Clover feel better, so instead, she held Clover's dirty, little hand and tried to smile.

"*We're* family now."

Clover leaned over and gave Lennox a hug. Her little head rested on Lennox's shoulder as she sat on the bench until another whistle blew. It was time to go back to work.

Chapter 22

The Regime soldiers made the prisoners work until nightfall, then marched the prisoners back to their lodging. Defiers staggered in line behind Thompson. Lennox looked at him from an entirely new perspective. He was the worst of the worst. It took a lot for Lennox *not* to hate him. She wanted to see him suffer like he made Clover suffer, but she knew that was not the answer.

Thompson pressed them behind a secure fence and walked away without a word. It was unlike him to leave without throwing insults around like daggers. Lennox noticed the way he treated the other captives with blatant hatred. Now, he seemed odd, even odder than before. She wondered why he was called in the office. She originally thought he was reprimanded for his treatment of the prisoners, but now she doubted that.

A campfire glowed and flickered with the gentle

wind. Army-green canvas cots were lined up in rows. Lennox was surprised cots were provided for prisoners to sleep on. She sat down on one close to the fire and let the warmth of the flame make her sweat. The soft orange hue of the lights in the city looked peaceful in the distance.

The city turned her thoughts to Sky—which was bittersweet. She did not know whether to be furious or worry. Her heart would not free her mind from him. She had so many questions. How could he leave her behind? Why would he? What was he thinking? She did not understand his frame of mind. He was stronger and braver than she was. He would have come back for her by now. It did not make any sense for him to bow, like Ander had. He wouldn't have.

Lennox's fellow prisoners filled the cots around her. She looked for Clover, who ran to the cot next to hers. Clover tried to tell Lennox something. Her eyes were worried and her lips formed words, but Lennox could not understand what she warned her about.

Lennox turned around. Thompson stood behind her with a branding iron shaped like the infamous *D* within a circle. Lennox's heart pounded in her chest. She knew he was there for her. The pounding in her chest filled her ears, and her pulse raced through her veins. She wiped the sweat from her brow with her sleeve and blinked hard.

"Winters…" Thompson stood tall with his shoulders cocked back. Lennox stood to her feet with reluctance. "Take this branding iron and set it in the fire," he said with a smirk.

He enjoyed the pain of others too much. It sickened Lennox.

Her hand reached for the iron and she wrapped her fingers around the handle. Thompson jerked it back like they played a game. He found it amusing as he yanked her around like a rag doll. He let it go and she stumbled back. She hit the row of cots behind her.

The nerves in her hands shook wildly out of her control. She put the iron in the center of the fire, resting the handle on the edge. Lennox was tempted with the thought of hitting Thompson with the iron, but she refrained, knowing it would only make matters worse. She backed away from the heat and returned to her cot.

Thompson grabbed her by the back of her neck with force. "Wait."

She stood still as his fingers dug into her skin. The red flames floated around the metal iron. Thompson picked it up. The *D* glowed crimson. Sweat drenched Lennox's palms.

Two soldiers came from behind and held her in place. They startled her with their tenacity when they planted her feet to the ground with all their might and forced her to stretch out her arm. Their combined strength made it impossible for Lennox to squirm. Prisoners looked away and the grimaces on their faces told her this would hurt.

Thompson grabbed her exposed arm with his free hand. She grit her teeth to prepare for the pain, but nothing could prepare her for what she felt next.

The iron sizzled on her skin as rising smoke swirled around it. A moan escaped her lips. When the pain left her breathless, she crumbled to the dirt and held her arm.

The soldiers left her curled up in a ball next to the fire. They closed the fence behind them and joked with one another. Their laughter reminded Lennox of hyenas. They had no sympathy. Thompson threw the branding iron into a bucket of water outside the fence. Lennox watched the steam rise into the air. The sound sizzled the same as when it touched her skin.

The city's orange lights were fuzzy and brought Lennox no comfort. The burn on the inside of her forearm made her delirious. She mumbled unintelligible threats to Thompson, despite his absence.

Ryker and a woman named Rosie—who had served her in the cafeteria—dragged her to her cot. Lennox's feet trailed the dirt, leaving behind two lines. She wanted to vomit. Her body had not recovered from the isolation box, and the fresh burn sapped her remaining strength.

"Sleep," Ryker said with understanding.

They *all* understood. Lennox's body was too weak and dehydrated. Every prisoner remained quiet. The fire flickered through her eyelashes. Her eyes rolled to the back of her head. She was out, sound asleep.

When she opened her eyes, Clover stood over her. Lennox felt searing pain on her arm, followed by the cool touch of a damp piece of fabric on her forehead and neck. Clover—who had torn her oversized jumpsuit—wiped away the dirt and sweat from Lennox's face with soft, sweeping motions. Clover had removed her stitches, too.

"How long have I been out?" Lennox asked somewhat confused. It was still night.

"A full day." Clover poured more water from her

canteen onto the dirty fabric.

A full day was unthinkable. Lennox was surprised the soldiers let her skip a day of work. They were not ones to care about the pain of another. Defiers were barely above animals to them.

"They let me miss work?" Lennox's facial features squished together when she furrowed her brows. Something must have happened.

"A small group of Sparrows was captured. They made the guards forget about you for a little while," Clover said.

"Sparrows?" Hope wilted in Lennox's soul. "Where are they?" Lennox tried to prop herself up on her arms, but her left arm collapsed. "Ouch!" she murmured.

She looked down at her bloodied arm. Burn blisters had formed and oozed yellow liquid. A raised scar would soon take their place. Lennox noticed the scar on Clover's arm. Her scar was still pink and tender. She could not imagine Clover's twelve-year-old little body enduring the same pain.

Clover lifted Lennox's head and gave her a sip of water.

"They should be here soon." Clover looked at the gate. Her blonde hair fell from underneath her cap and spilled onto her face. She looked like a sweet angel who suffered something terrible and cruel.

Lennox held Clover's hand as she sat on her cot. Lennox was sure she must look pitiful. She fixed her gaze on the entrance of the prison gate. They watched and waited for the Sparrows to walk in.

Who they saw next sent sharp pangs through Lennox's chest.

It was Ander.

Chapter 23

Coward, hypocrite, enemy, and *traitor* were the words that came to mind when Lennox saw him.

Ander took Lennox by the elbow and led her out of the gate. The black fatigues he wore tortured her. How could he *already* be a Regime soldier? He violated Lennox's trust and sympathy, and betrayed his faith. He sickened her.

Lennox kept her head down. She could not stand to see his face. Ander took her to the same office the suited man went to previously. He sat Lennox on a wooden stool by the guard who was behind the desk in front of her.

"Wait here." It was the first sentence Ander spoke to her since he bowed.

Her arm throbbed with a pulsing sensation that ran from her elbow to her wrist. She watched as the guard cracked sunflower seeds between his teeth and spit them out. Drool ran down his chin. She was disgusted. When he looked away, she made sure her locket was tucked underneath the collar of her jumpsuit.

She looked out the window to see the other prisoners. They worked… as usual.

Ander returned and led Lennox to a darkened room with one bright light. It was an interrogation room. The gray walls looked like tombstones. A two-way mirror reflected Lennox's image back at her. She didn't even look like herself. Her face showed the signs of stress and brown dirt was smudged against her usually clean skin. There was a steel table in the middle of the room with chairs on opposing sides.

The suited man entered. He was about the same height as Sky. His auburn hair was slicked back and his skin was pulled tight. His cologne masked the scent of smoke that followed him. He took off his jacket and put it on the back of the chair that was in front of the mirror. Lennox thought he looked familiar.

"Sit down," he insisted. Ander pulled the chair out for Lennox. She scoffed at the gesture. "That's right. You two know each other." The man seemed pleased.

"No, we don't," Lennox said, wishing she could punch Ander square in the face. She clenched her jaw.

Ander's eyes fell to the floor and his features tightened.

"Well, I beg to differ. I think you two know each other quite well. I brought him in here with you because you *do* know each other. I thought he could talk some sense into you," the man said.

If only he knew. She met Ander only a few days ago. Ander had no power over her—or her decisions.

The man tried to look soft and inviting so Lennox would be more willing to open up to him, but instead, he appeared creepy.

"Do you know who I am, child?" he asked. He put his chin down to his chest and raised his eyebrows.

"No, sir, I don't," Lennox answered honestly.

It did not matter to her who he was, all she knew was she did not want to be in the same room with him. He gave her the same, chilling feeling as the Prowler's faceless man.

"I am Commander Ahab, Head of the Regime," he said with a sinister grin of achievement plastered on his face.

Lennox felt sickened by his pride. How could he be so proud? His cruelty ruined countless lives. His legacy was death. Humanity had left him long ago. He sat back in his chair and folded his leg over the other, waiting for a response from her.

"So you are the one responsible for my parents' deaths," she said bluntly. The response was not the one he wanted.

The necklace slid into view and the light caught the gold locket around her neck. It glimmered, shining a small light in the dull gray room. Ahab noticed and stood abruptly. He ripped it from around her neck. Lennox felt her hands curl into tense fists and she reached for the locket.

"Give it back!" She stood to her feet, pushing the chair out from under her and shoving the table with her legs. She lunged, but was subdued by Ander.

Lennox could not understand how Ander could defend or protect the very man who caused him so much loss. She scowled when he forced her to stay seated and held his strong hands on her shoulders, pinning her to the chair.

Lennox had to get the locket back. Her mind raced as she tried to think of a way to rip it from Ahab's hands and flee.

"I see we have a fighter on our hands," Ahab laughed, making his way back to his chair. He shoved the necklace in his pocket as if he took nothing from her.

Did he know what the locket was? Maybe he only wanted to get a rise out of her. Whatever his intentions, it did not matter. She despised him and knew she had to get it back.

He leaned forward and rested his elbows on top of the table. His hand reached for Lennox's wrist and strangled it in his grasp while his other hand slapped the fresh *D* on her arm. Lennox pulled back, wincing with pain. Ander flinched and looked at her with pity. She despised him for it. She prayed within her heart for the Lord to give her courage.

Commander Ahab stood and whispered something in Ander's ear. Ander walked out of the room, leaving Lennox alone with this terrible man. There was a long strain of silence as Ahab stared at her until Ander barged back into the room.

Lennox's leather satchel hit the table and its contents spilled out. Her only possessions scattered to the floor and table. Commander Ahab picked them up and threw them on the table as he shuffled his fingers through each one of her belongings. His hand lingered on the Bible. He slammed it on the table. The blow assaulted her ears and she jumped back in her chair.

"Don't you know this leather bound book is a relic and illegal to have in your possession?" Spit flew from Commander Ahab's mouth.

"If it is a relic, then why are you so afraid of it?" Lennox found her courage. Perhaps she should have asked for wisdom as well.

The Commander darted around the table and pushed Ander out of the way. He shoved Lennox's nose into the leather bound book that he feared.

"Deny the words in this book, or you will be my prisoner forever," he said through pursed lips too close to Lennox's ear for comfort.

She softly uttered a response. "You can imprison my flesh, but you can never imprison my soul. The Lord frees my heart every morning. He comforts me and protects me every night." She knew those words might be her last, but she would stand behind them. They were true.

"God has not done a good job then, has He?" Ahab laughed with delight, shaking his head. "You are a fool, girl. You will never be free." He let the disgusted pleasure of Lennox's choice roll over his face. He would spend time trying to break her, which he took pleasure in. "Your faith will be the death of you!" he spit again.

"My faith is what makes me alive," Lennox retorted, locking her eyes with his. She refused to let him intimidate her.

He shook his head with a stupid, sinister grin. His smoky cologne made her gag as he returned to his chair.

"Tell me where Sparrow City is… and maybe… I will let you live."

Lennox relished the silence. Did he not see the map in her bag?

"Fine, have it your way. I'm going to let you live just so you can see the rest of your world fall. I have only just begun ripping your world apart, and I won't stop until I have broken you—and it—completely." His eyes grew colder and more demented. "Give her ten lashes for her sedition and throw her back with the others. She is of no use to me. Burn all of her belongings with everyone else's, she won't be needing them anymore."

Ander led Lennox back through the office and past the guard with the sunflower seeds. Drool still dripped from his chin. The prisoners no longer worked outside the window. Lennox's feelings for Sky flooded her brain. They were muddied and confused. She loved him, and she despised him at the same time.

How could he leave me behind?

She looked at Ander to see if any of the little she knew about the old him was still there. Was there any part of him left? Was there any fight for faith remaining?

She looked at Ander and searched for remnants of his faith, but his eyes lacked compassion as he led her through the gate.

She strained to see Ander as he slid her back through the prison gate. He nodded his head, making sure she saw him. Maybe he was sorry for the ten lashes he gave her on her back, but it did not seem like he was sorry at all. She wanted an explanation for why he joined the Regime. She prayed there was a rational reason for his irrational behavior, but nothing made sense except his need to save his own skin. He did not care who he hurt in the process. She had to hope for his sake—and her own—that there was a better reason for his cowardice, but she knew there wasn't.

Lennox's cot had a small white daisy placed on it. She was sure Clover left it for her.

Prisoners were clumped together as far away from the gate as they could get. Lennox assumed they did not want the guards to hear their conversation as Ryker talked with their new prisoners—the captured Sparrows.

Lennox strained her steps to meet them. It was Cameron's team. Cameron saw Lennox running toward them and met her halfway. She greeted her with a hug. Lennox flinched from pain as Cameron's hand brushed against her freshly wounded back.

"Cameron, I can't believe you all are here." Lennox ignored the blood that trickled down her spine.

"We are going to get you all out of here," Cameron whispered with hope written all over her face. After all, the Sparrows had escaped before. *She* had escaped before.

Lennox touched the base of her neck and wanted to cry. "The necklace is gone. Ahab took it during my interrogation."

Cameron eyed Lennox's neck. "I will get it back. I should have never left you alone with it in the first place," she said, squeezing Lennox's shoulder. "Trust me, I will get it back."

Lennox inhaled and shook her head. She felt like she had failed and wanted to rewind. Thoughts of fighting harder to get it back set her heart ablaze, adding fuel to her escape mission.

As they got closer to the crowd, Cameron walked to the middle of the prisoners. She had their full attention and respect as she mapped out a plan. Clover's hand gripped Lennox's. She pulled Lennox close and looked up in an attempt to read her thoughts, just as Lennox had tried to read Ander's. Lennox smiled with the reassurance this was their best bet. If anyone could get them out of prison, it was Cameron and her team. They finally had a plan and a leader who was willing to risk it all to free every prisoner.

"There are more of us than there are of them. Our next work detail, we can overtake them and get the keys to the gates," Cameron told the men in the group.

"Then what? What will we do when we get outside the gates? We don't have any gear or weapons," Ryker said. He previously planned an unsuccessful escape and lost good men. Lennox knew he did not want to lose anyone else. None of them did.

"We will have to worry about that when we get to that point. I am sure they still have all of our Sparrow tech locked up in their offices. We will have to break in and get it back," Cameron said.

Lennox jumped in, "I just came from the offices. I know the layout, but they had my stuff too. They are going to burn everything tonight."

There was no way they could execute this plan in time. Their next work detail in the ditch was in the morning. All their belongings would be ash by then.

"Then we have to use their gear," Cameron reinforced.

She was going through with this plan, no matter what. Everyone nodded in agreement. The Sparrows knew what they were doing. They were trained for war, and the Defiers would trust in that training.

Throughout the night, clusters of men, women, and teenagers huddled together and whispered. The prison camp's atmosphere felt different. A spark ignited, and the flames of hope would burn down the walls that held them in.

Chapter 24

Every prisoner rose early, way before work detail. Thompson stood guard earlier than he normally would, and Lennox noticed there were more guards than usual.

Something was wrong. The guards knew something was happening. They did not converse with one another and jokes were not exchanged. Their focus was on the Defiers. Every prisoner was closely monitored. The guards' eyes scanned the premises as they walked along the perimeter of the fence, never losing focus.

Other prisoners started to notice that something was wrong too. Ryker and Cameron found each other. They rethought escape plans, trying to adjust to the seriousness of the guards.

Commander Ahab made an unexpected appearance from one of the barracks. His suit more polished than the last he wore. It was lined with blood-red silk and was complimented by a starched black shirt that buttoned around his neck. The hem of his tailored suit pants were dusty. He walked at a casual pace toward the prison gate with his alligator skin shoes. Thompson and two others followed behind him.

The two new guards that flanked Commander Ahab were bigger and stronger than Thompson. They also seemed more experienced. They were presumably his new detail.

"I heard there were plans being made to escape," Ahab stated as a matter of fact. "Don't you know you can't escape here? No prisoner ever has, and no prisoner ever will." He gave a ferocious laugh and looked at Cameron. "You are not special, Miss Cameron, and your Sparrows are not special." He spit in her face.

Cameron wiped her brow with the back of her hand. "We will see about that." She stared at Ahab, giving him no room for intimidation.

Commander Ahab's cheeks grew red with rage as he demanded respect. "Throw them in the chambers! All of them!" he shouted.

The word *chambers* did not sound pleasant to Lennox.

The guards obeyed and charged the prisoners. They pointed their guns, demanding they form a line. Then they shackled their feet together with iron chains. Clover was in front of Lennox with another woman in front of her.

Cameron was forced to lead. The chains clanked as they walked past the ditch, past the offices, and two miles farther.

The prisoner procession stopped and stood in front of a large, windowless, cement building located near the industrial city. It reminded Lennox of the isolation box at the prison camp. Clover began to cry as the soldiers led them inside. Her shackles rubbed her ankles raw.

"It's going to be okay, Clover. Hang in there." Lennox tried to encourage her.

When the reinforcements arrived, the guards outnumbered the Defiers. It seemed like the Regime was always one step ahead. Lennox wondered if their whispering the night before was the reason their escape plan was discovered. She guessed it did not matter anymore. The fact was, the Regime found out, and now the Defiers were in a windowless prison with no fresh air.

Thompson unchained their feet without eye contact. Every guard slowly backed out of the cement box. Their guns were aimed at them until they cleared the vault door that only opened from outside. The locks slid into place one by one. Lennox counted at least ten locks. The final lock echoed off the cold, gray walls.

At first, everyone remained quiet. Then the chatter started. New strategies were formed. Cameron, along with her team, brainstormed new ways to escape their new prison. These four cement walls were much different than the electrified chain link fence. They would be much harder to escape.

Scattered lights hung from the ceiling that stood at least fifty feet above them. The room looked like a former warehouse of some kind. The Regime had only recently cleared it out to be used as a prison. Vents sat high on the walls. Lennox watched as a thick yellow fog seeped through them.

The talking ceased.

"We are in a gas chamber," Ryker said, lifting his undershirt over his mouth and nose.

"Everyone cover your faces!" Cameron shouted.

Clover rested her head close to Lennox's chest as her sleeve covered her little face. Lennox pulled her own sleeve over her hand and held it to her nose, breathing through the musty fabric. It would not be enough to stop the gas from reaching their lungs.

"Take as small of breaths as you can," Lennox urged Clover, knowing it would do no good. Lennox watched as her little pupils glazed over.

Rosie sang an old hymn under her breath. As the fog grew thicker, her voice got louder.

Rosie previously told Lennox she was a gospel singer. She sang every week at her church before the war... before it was shut down. After that, the congregation met at Rosie's house, which was how she was captured. People flocked to her home one Sunday morning when Regime soldiers broke down her front door. They set her house on fire. Only she and a few others briefly escaped, then they were caught. The brutal soldiers beat them and then threw them into the prison camp. A few tears ran down Rosie's face when she told Lennox her story, but Rosie wiped them away and said she relied on God when she did not understand why or how. She had built a foundation of trust in the Lord that would not be stolen, and she encouraged Lennox to do the same.

Rosie's voice was as smooth and strong as the faith she demonstrated. Her tune bounced from wall to wall, making her voice multiply into a choir. Lennox concentrated on the words she sang. They brought her a little peace and comfort.

Lennox wrapped her other hand around Clover as the gas made them weak. She leaned her back against the gray cement and slid her body's weight down. Clover slid down with her. Cameron tried to stand beside them but fell to her knees. She rested her head on the floor.

Lennox did not know what to do. She still had faith in God. Her spirit reminded her that He was with them, but it was hard to get her flesh to do anything of faith. The gas clouded her judgment. Her eyelids closed off her vision. She heard faint whispers in the distance, Rosie's singing stopped. She was unsure of what was happening. Maybe this was the end.

The gas subsided and the yellow fog disappeared. Lennox's body was no longer weak. Clover woke up next to her, surprised she still breathed. Cameron stood up, holding her hands to her head.

"What was that all about?" she asked.

"I have no idea," Lennox said. She thought it was strange they all survived a gas chamber. The Regime must have made a mistake and used the wrong gas.

They met Ryker in the middle of the room.

"Sir, do you know what that was?" Cameron asked him.

"I am not sure, I've never seen anything like it," Ryker said, shaking his head.

One by one, the door locks unbolted. The heavy door swung open. The sun pierced through and filled the room with natural light. Guards marched in. Commander Ahab stepped through them with his usual, sinister grin. Lennox's lungs felt tight when she breathed the outdoor air.

"You are feeling the effects of the gas, aren't you?" Ahab walked to Lennox and lifted up her chin. "I dare you to try to escape now. I will show you what happens if you do."

Ahab pulled Cameron outside the door. Her breaths turned violent and her lips turned blue. Her body hit the earth. Her hands dug into the dirt as she struggled to breathe. She took huge gasps, searching for a clean source of oxygen. Lennox watched helplessly as Cameron fought. She could not stand there and watch her die.

"Let her go!" she cried.

She ran too close to the open door. Her hands grabbed

her throat, choking on the fresh air. They had not poisoned the air… they poisoned their lungs.

She saw Ander step around one of the bigger guards he hid behind. He pushed her back into the chamber. She looked at him with her hands still wrapped around her throat. Her lungs burned. She looked down at Cameron, then back at Ander, silently pleading for him to help.

He could do nothing until Commander Ahab left.

"Your lungs can only survive in the chambers," Ahab explained. "Outside of these walls, you will meet your deaths. You will be working in the chambers from now on, building the very weapons that will decimate your beloved Sparrows. You will receive one slice of bread and one cup of water per day. That's it. You have worn out my generosity."

Commander Ahab stepped over Cameron as he returned to his vehicle. Ander waited until he drove off before he rolled Cameron through the life and death barrier. Then he left with the other guards and pulled the door closed.

"Cameron," Lennox leaned her ear to her face, searching for breath.

Blood drained from Cameron's ears and mouth. Everyone gathered around her and prayed. Lennox did the same. She *had* to live. Lennox would not accept any more death.

Cameron's lips turned from blue to a pale flesh color. Short staggered coughs jerked her body. The color of her skin normalized as her dark eyes stared at the ceiling. She was going to make it.

Lennox looked at her fellow prisoners. Their hearts were as heavy as her own. They were trapped. Their very bodies fought against escape. They had to face it. There was no escaping with the poison in their lungs. The oxygen outside the chamber walls meant certain death.

Chapter 25

It was hard to tell when night fell behind the chamber's walls, but Lennox knew it was close to dusk. The lights flickered for a while, and then went out. Maybe this was the signal to go to sleep. No one knew the rules for these unfamiliar quarters.

The clicks of the opening locks shocked the inhabitants. The group did not expect to see the door open again so soon. Lennox readied for a fight. She stood protectively over Clover as she slept. The darkness was blinding, but her other senses were fully aware. As the door cracked open, a lone man's silhouette came into view. His shape was framed by the glowing city lights. As he stepped closer, the moon's small, silver light fell on his face, shining through the opening. Lennox recognized him.

"Sky…"

The light made him look older. His high cheekbones

cast a shadow on the rest of his features. He placed a rock between the door and shined a flashlight. Prisoners stood to their feet. They looked ready to attack. A man bolted with vengeance.

"Stop!" Lennox yelled. "I know him! He is my friend."

The man stopped in his tracks. He held his hand to his mouth, coughing from the fresh air.

The beam of light found her face.

"Lennox?"

She ran. She wrapped her arms around his neck and he hugged her waist as he lifted her off the ground and kissed her cheek.

"I'm so sorry, I tried to get to you sooner, but I couldn't," he said as tears welled up in his eyes. He set her back down, gently.

"How'd you escape?" Lennox asked, not really caring how. She was just glad he did.

"I was trapped in the soldier bunker when the anthem played. I changed into a soldier uniform, but by the time I returned, you and Ander were gone. I found Ander in the city in uniform too. He told me everything. I'm so sorry he left you alone. I'm sorry for leaving you with him. I wanted to kill him for it." Sky held his head low with disappointment.

"It's okay, it made me stronger." Lennox raised his head and gave him a small smile. She could not stay mad at him forever.

Sky noticed the *D* on her arm and winced in pain.

"I'm okay, just a flesh wound," she reassured him. Good thing he didn't see the lashes on her back. He would be furious.

"I made Ander tell me where you were. He gave me the keys to the chambers after a little fight."

A *little fight* to Sky meant he threw a few hard punches. Lennox was not sure if Ander felt bad for what he had done, but she knew if Sky was *that* angry, he could have gotten anything simply by overpowering him. Ander made his choice, just like she made hers. He would live with it for the rest of his life. Lennox knew her father's words were true, now more than ever. "If you don't surrender to God, you will surrender to man." He told her that phrase often, which was a part of the reason she chose to stand.

Lennox looked at Sky. "We can't leave the chambers. They poisoned our lungs."

He held up a bag and then handed it to her. "They're inhalers. Get all of the prisoners to take them. They will deactivate the poison and trackers in your systems. You have to get ready to run." His eyes were wide with determination, like that night in the woods when he jumped out from behind the tree. He must have made another difficult decision.

Cameron helped distribute the inhalers. Lennox gave Clover one before she took her own. Clover inhaled the contents with a deep breath. Lennox followed suit and stuck the medication to her mouth and inhaled. A blast of medicine saturated their lungs, cleansing the poison from their systems. Lennox tested the results by walking close to the cracked door. The fresh, natural oxygen invigorated her.

She faced Cameron—who assisted everyone else with their treatment—and forced her to take hers. Once everyone was treated, they walked through the opened door.

Finally! They were free.

Lennox followed Cameron as she walked toward Sky and Ryker.

"You all need to leave, now. Take everyone to Sparrow City," Cameron instructed.

"What about you? Where are you going to go?" Lennox interjected before she remembered Cameron's promise to retrieve the locket.

"I'm going to get the microchip."

"How are you going to do that by yourself?" Sky asked. "The city has guards all around it, doesn't it?"

"It does, but we need that locket and my team. I have to leave right now to get it while we still have the element of surprise on our side. Plus, we have to find a way to disable the GWS in this location if you all are going to make it," Cameron said, motioning for a few Sparrows to accompany her. "Get them to safety."

Sky and Lennox watched as Cameron sprinted into the woods. They knew their long-term survival depended on her success.

"We have to get the rest of the people out of here." Lennox rubbed her forehead. "I don't have the map anymore. They burned my stuff."

Sky took her by the hand and led a few steps further. He picked up a bag from the dirt and dusted it off, then handed it to her. He must have saved it before it was incinerated. She opened it. The map and her Bible were still inside.

"How did you—?"

"Trust me, you don't want to know," Sky said, grabbing the map. He unfolded the paper and checked their coordinates. "Looks like we are not that far away."

He bit his lower lip.

"How far are we?" Lennox asked with uncertainty. Could it really be this close to a Regime stronghold?

"The map says we are about twenty-eight miles away," Sky said, tracing the line.

"That's impossible! Wouldn't the Regime know its location, then?"

A realization hit her. Commander Ahab saw the contents of her bag. He must have seen the map to Sparrow City. He had the locket. He had everything.

"Oh, no…" Lennox covered her face with her hands.

"What is it?" Sky asked.

"It's Ahab. He had to have seen the map when he went through my bag, and he must know where we are going and what route we are taking. He asked me to tell him where it was, but I refused, hoping that he would overlook the map. He had to have seen it. I just know it!"

"Then we better move fast." Sky put his pack on and ran back through the chamber door.

Lennox followed. They looked at the people who depended on them for their escape. Everyone's face was bright with renewed hope as Sky became the leader he was destined to be.

"Listen, everyone!" He commanded. "We have to get

out of here fast. We think the Regime knows the location of Sparrow City. We have to leave while we still have a chance."

Clover ran beside Lennox and held her hand.

"We are finally going to get you out of here," Lennox whispered with a soft smile.

Clover nodded and squeezed Lennox's hand tighter.

Sky led the way as Ryker stayed back to warn of any pursuing soldiers. Clover and Lennox moved their feet swiftly over the earth to stay right behind Sky. If everyone maintained this pace, they might make it to Sparrow City before the Regime even knew they were gone.

Lennox hoped Cameron could disable the GWS and get the locket back in time. It was the only way to ensure the climate was safe for everyone. They hoped to avoid all unwanted surprises.

Traveling deeper and deeper in the woods, they barely saw the orange glow of the industrial city. The lights flickered in the distance, and then completely disappeared. Raging, orange flames replaced them. The city was on fire. The blaze echoed crackling noises through the woods, and the smell of smoke drifted near their location. Cameron and the Sparrows must have shut down the GWS.

Sky walked faster, following the map. The prisoners marched steadily behind him.

This was it. They would finally make it.

Clover held tight to Lennox's hand as they rushed over branches and rocks. The flames became a distant haze.

After several miles, older Defiers became weary and their bodies ached for rest. Lennox pulled at Sky's pack and showed him how they struggled. Even Clover's little feet barely held her up. Sky stopped, acknowledging their need for rest. Ryker ran from the back to talk to him.

"We can only let them rest for a few minutes—thirty at the most. The Regime is bound to be after us," Ryker said as sweat poured from his brow.

Sky and Lennox nodded in agreement. They could let the tired Defiers catch their breath and rest their feet—but only for a short time.

Chapter 26

Day woke. Birds flew above them in the early morning sky. Their songs echoed with vibrancy through the branches. Lennox hummed their songs back to them, making Clover smile. She tried to forget that drones or soldiers could find them at any minute. Just a few more miles and they would be at Sparrow City— where there was a safe place to stay and freedom from the threat of attack.

They walked through the trees and into a clearing where hills rolled for miles. The map indicated that Sparrow City was underground and hidden behind hills. They were close. If hope were a taste, Lennox salivated for it. She anticipated the moment when she no longer had to look over her shoulder for pursuing soldiers, drones, or Prowlers.

The grass that reached Lennox's waist waved in the wind as they hiked over the rolling hills.

Lennox heard the sound she learned to dread. Commander Ahab had found them. Drones hovered over them like daunting storm clouds. Lennox waited for their lightning to strike—the inevitable bombs the Regime loved to drop—but it never came. Instead, the earth rumbled beneath their feet.

At first, it was a soft shake. Then it rumbled harder. The shaking grew fierce like an earthquake. Lennox assumed the Regime must have found a way to reactivate the GWS. The ground began to separate violently from itself. Lennox reached for Clover and her fingertips barely held on. The earthquake pulled them apart as Clover's hand slipped from Lennox's grasp.

"Hold on!" Lennox shouted.

She hurled her body over the huge chasm that separated them. The earth tore itself further apart with every shake. Clover slipped and fell down a crevice that quickly appeared. Lennox caught her just before the earth could consume her.

She hugged her body to the trembling dirt and laid flat on her stomach, her hands clung to Clover's tiny wrists. Lennox was desperate to anchor her feet to something, but nothing held. She started to slip down. Flailing her feet into the dirt, Lennox's body inched over the wide opening as the earth continued to shake beneath her. The muscles in her arms flexed tighter. Her fingers gripped harder. The earth's violent shaking was relentless.

"It's going to be okay. Don't let go!" Lennox held onto Clover with all of her might.

She scanned the perimeter. The Sparrows struggled to help everyone to safety. Sky held someone the same way Lennox grasped Clover. There was no one to help. She knew she could not do it on her own. Lennox turned her focus back as sweat dripped from her face onto Clover's.

"Lord, help us," Lennox prayed with faith, knowing that only God could save them.

Lennox pulled with a surge of strength, but her energy drained fast. She had enough strength to position her body so it no longer hung over the edge.

She heard a dog bark behind her, but she could not turn to see it without losing her grip. Lennox thought the Regime had caught up to them and thought that the dog would be their end.

A furry body pushed next to Lennox and a canine's teeth sunk into the sleeve of Clover's jumpsuit. The dog tried to pull Clover up. Their combined strength and weight helped to pull Clover's shoulders over the crumbling ledge. The earth still shook, but not as violently as before. Lennox felt herself regain control. She pulled with her last bit of strength. The dog planted its haunches and tugged. With one final pull, Clover lay next to her. Lennox squeezed her tight in her tired arms.

"Are you okay?" Lennox asked. The thought of losing her made Lennox tremble. She did not want to lose anyone else.

Clover nodded her head, "Yes." She was too out of breath to speak.

Lennox looked at the animal that helped rescue Clover. It was a German shepherd with a patch of white fur on its chin. Lennox's heart leaped out of her chest.

"Grizzly! Is that you?"

She pulled the dog's furry body close and kissed her. Grizzly licked Lennox's cheek with recognition. She knew that if Grizzly was here, that meant there was a good chance that Oliver was, too. Her heart skipped a beat as she spun in circles trying to find him. Grizzly barked at her. Lennox grabbed Clover and ran, following the dog to the safety of the other Defiers. Grizzly sprinted off to help others. Her K9 training taught her to pull people to safety on her own.

Lennox's heart dropped when she remembered Sky. She turned to see if he had made it out, but saw he still clung to someone. Before Lennox could assist him, an unknown Sparrow ran and grabbed hold of the person's right hand and helped Sky pull them up. Ryker's face emerged from the hole in the ground. Sky had been trying to pull his massive body up by himself.

The earthquake finally stopped. Lennox sighed with a faint breath of relief and bent over with her hands on her knees. Her eyes searched for Oliver. The Sparrow pointed Ryker toward the crowd, but when Sky saw the Sparrow's face, he tackled him with a hug. Then, Lennox realized who it was.

"Oliver!"

He was unrecognizable from where Lennox stood, but there was no doubt it was him. Her feet leapt high over the broken earth as she ran past the cracks to where they were. Lennox wrapped her arms around him in an exuberant embrace. Oliver had found his way to them. He was alive, and he was there with her. His skin had aged and a beard hid his face, but it was him. Lennox's brother was an answered prayer.

"Thank you, Lord," spilled from her lips. It was unbelievable how they were brought back together.

"How did you know where to find us?" Lennox asked. Her voice was high pitched with amazement.

"I was just returning from a mission when my crew saw the drones over the hills," he answered.

Sky, Oliver, and Lennox huddled together. Their reunion was a blessing that they would not take for granted. No matter what storm came their way, they could weather it together. One day at a time.

Grizzly and the other K9s growled at the distant trees as if they warned of an attack. They ran to the other Sparrows and Defiers. As the Regime approached, the dogs' warnings grew louder. Blind shots were fired from the tree line. Bullets buried themselves in the hillside, too close to Sky's head. He heard it whiz by him and his eyes widened.

"What do we do?" Lennox asked, turning to Oliver and Sky.

"Run to Sparrow City as fast as you can. Take all of them with you." Oliver pointed to the rest of the Defiers.

The Regime continued to advance. The Sparrows from Oliver's crew took the frontlines with their shields and weapons drawn. Bullets ricocheted with pinging sounds off of their Sapphire Shields. Sky activated his own and shouted for everyone to run. The multitude sprinted up the hill in clumps, but Lennox stopped her in her tracks.

Ahab's amplified voice came from the speakers of a Humvee. "Hand over the 'girl who stood,' and we will give you not one... but four of your men."

Lennox turned around and saw the Humvee pull to a stop on top of a hill. Cameron and the other Sparrows were dragged out of the vehicle and forced to their knees.

"You have my word." Ahab continued. "If you give us the girl, we will give you these Sparrows and leave Sparrow City alone."

Lennox started to walk down the hill, but Sky grabbed her sleeve. "Lennox, don't. You know his word means nothing."

"He still has the locket and he is going to kill them if I don't go," she said, loosing Sky's hand. She wrapped her arms around him. "I love you."

She had waited so long to tell him those three small words.

Sky whispered sweetly back, "I love you, too. That's why I can't let you do this."

"You *have* to let me do this."

Ahab grew impatient and fired a shot. A Sparrow's

body crumpled to the ground. Lennox's heart sank as she pulled herself away from Sky. She sprinted.

Sky hollered for Oliver, and they both ran to catch her.

Oliver reached out, catching her sleeve.

"Lennox, you can't! They'll kill you. Besides, they could never break into Sparrow City even if they knew exactly where it was. There is a force field that only Sparrow tech can pass." Oliver gripped her wrists.

"That doesn't help, Cameron!" Lennox stared him in the eyes. "It didn't help the Sparrow Ahab just killed. I can't let anyone else die! I can stop it. It's my fault they're captured. I didn't keep the locket safe."

His hands fell from her wrists like when she ran to the silo, but this time, she was not running away. She faced the challenges of life head on. She hugged him one last time as he frantically tried to change her mind. Then she shoved him away and ran as fast as she could.

As she approached the clearing, she slowed to a walk with her hands held above her head. She looked over her shoulder. Sky and Oliver were close behind, but shots were fired to keep them in their place. When Ahab saw Lennox, he held his fist up and the Regime soldiers ceased firing.

Cameron saw Lennox walking toward them and shouted, "Lennox, you don't have to do this!" A rifle butt met her jaw and she was knocked to the side. Her left hand kept her from falling completely.

Lennox did not want to do this. She *had* to do this. She could not—would not—let anyone else die for her. She had to stand up for her faith and the people that she loved. It was the only thing in the world that made sense to her anymore. She remembered a verse about how there is no greater love than a man laying down his life for his friends. It gave her strength.

As she got closer, a Regime soldier ran to meet her. He grabbed her by the arm and walked her up the hill to Ahab. She did not understand why he wouldn't just kill her already and get it over with. Ahab released Cameron and the two other Sparrows as they got closer.

When they passed by, Lennox nodded to them and uttered the phrase she previously thought she would never understand. "To live is gain and to die is gain."

Cameron's bruised face was covered with falling tears. She nodded in understanding. She could not deny the truth in that phrase. Her father was the one who told Lennox those exact words at the cabin. Cameron's jaw tightened and her eyebrows scrunched together as she looked over her shoulder.

Lennox was in God's hands now.

Chapter 27

Lord, make me brave.

Lennox needed courage more than ever before. It was one thing to be trapped with nowhere to go, but it was entirely different to freely walk into the enemy's camp.

The soldier threw her before Ahab like she was some sort of prize. There were no friends around her now. She looked up and saw that Ahab's face was dirty and his pressed suit was singed.

She smirked, with too much pleasure, perhaps. Ahab finally witnessed the true strength of the Sparrows and their capabilities. If they disabled the GWS and burned down a Regime stronghold once, they could do it again. Lennox hoped that maybe it showed him he was no god. Especially not hers.

Lennox's pleasure faded when she saw what was attached to the back of the Humvee. A clear, acrylic cage housed around five Prowlers. Ahab followed her stare and his face became delighted. He crouched down beside her and held her chin so she could not look away.

"One of my Prowlers told me you broke free of his hold."

Lennox did not even know Prowlers had the ability to speak. She had only heard them hiss.

Ahab continued, "I assure you, that won't happen again. Let's just say I gave them an upgrade." He forced Lennox to her feet. "Search her for weapons!"

Two soldiers patted at Lennox's clothes. They stopped when they found an adaptor blade shoved in her left boot that she had covered with her pants. A soldier took it and handed it to Ahab.

"Nice try, little girl," the soldier spat.

Lennox heard the shouts from the Sparrows, but they could do nothing except watch.

Ahab walked her to the clear door of the cage. The Prowlers clawed at the acrylic. Their alien eyes lingered on her as if she was their next meal. A soldier near the back of the cage pushed a button, releasing a gas that subdued the Prowlers. They appeared comatose. Another soldier opened the cage door and Ahab shoved Lennox inside.

"Let's see how you do against five of them, shall

we?" Ahab slammed the cage door and locked it in place. "Wake them up," he commanded.

Lennox banged on the smooth, bulletproof wall. A soldier hit the button on the outside of the cage and the Prowlers began to stir. She lifted her head and took slow, calming breaths. One by one they stood to their feet and locked their sights on her.

She felt helpless. She had to overcome the fear that tried to crawl with it. She needed faith. It could override everything she felt at that moment. She had to fully trust God with her mind, body, and soul, or else they would grab hold of her. She had to surrender to Christ completely. He would deliver her. Even if He didn't, He was still her Savior and her Deliverer.

Faith crawled through her veins like fire, keeping her on her feet. She closed her eyes so that she could see— really see—with her spirit. She envisioned Christ was in the cage with her. She was learning how to trust like never before.

The Prowlers tried to grab hold of her thoughts, but there was no room for them anymore. She lifted her hands over her head in praise. She was free from their mind games. Christ was her redemption and her salvation. She knew without any doubt that Jesus Christ was with her just as He was with Daniel in the lion's den. He was with her the same as with Shadrach, Meshach, and Abednego in the fiery furnace.

When the Prowlers realized their psychological war was ineffective, they came at her with their physical strength, but that failed as well. It was as if a radioactive explosion took place within the cage. Lennox opened her eyes and saw the Prowlers debilitated on the clear floor.

Without warning, the walls of the acrylic cage shattered and acrylic daggers flew toward the Regime.

Ahab fell to his knees in the grass in disbelief. He let out a haunting scream with his hands on his head and his fingers pulling at his hair.

"Kill her, I want her dead!" Ahab shouted with a roar, his eyes were cold like a snake's.

The sound of a helicopter made Lennox look up. Sparrows from Sparrow City had arrived. A ladder fell from the helicopter, its end five feet in front of Lennox. She grabbed hold and began to climb as it flew to safety.

Bullets flew and drones chased, but they were incapacitated by Sparrow technology. Lennox watched as drones were incinerated when they flew into the invisible force field Oliver referenced. She looked back from the safety of the helicopter's interior and saw Ahab wave his fists in the air, commanding his soldiers to regain control of the Defiers that were on the ground.

The soldiers got close and Lennox cringed when one almost snagged Clover off her feet.

"No!" she screamed.

A female Sparrow inside the helicopter held Lennox back from the opening so that she would not fall.

"We have to help them," Lennox pleaded.

"Look," the Sparrow smiled. Her pale skin and brown eyes were soft and reassuring.

Lennox watched as Oliver swung Clover onto his back and ran to a large chasm. Sky was beside him, helping the older Defiers.

"There's nowhere for them to go. It's a drop-off." Lennox said, staring into the Sparrows unworried eyes.

The Sparrow pointed down once again, and Lennox was left breathless. She was awestruck as she watched pieces of earth rise and collide together. The pieces of rock molded into place, making a perfect bridge for hundreds of people to walk on. It appeared to hang from nothing as they floated in the air. She watched in amazement at what she knew was the work of the Lord. With man, this was impossible, but with God, all things were possible. With God, they moved mountains. This was not how it was going to end.

God had a plan for them. All of them. He always had one.

Rocks stretched as far as her eyes could see. Oliver took the first step onto the floating pathway with Clover still on his back. The rest of the Defiers followed. When the last Defier crossed the floating pathway, the stones fell back down into the earth's cavity.

The Regime soldiers that followed close behind slid to a stop and fired their weapons. Their bullets ricocheted off of the invisible force field.

"That's amazing!" Lennox shouted.

"Yes, it is," her Sparrow companion smiled.

The helicopter flew faster and went straight through the force field unharmed. It landed on a grassy hill next to a large, steel-gray door built into the rounded hill.

"Welcome to Sparrow City. I'm Easton." The Sparrow took off her helmet and released her straight, dark hair.

Lennox saw the scar that ran from left to right across her beautiful face.

She shook her hand. "I'm Lennox."

Easton's smile reached her eyes. "I know who you are, 'girl who stood.'" Easton patted Lennox on the shoulder then walked to the other side of the helicopter to talk to the pilot.

Lennox was beginning to like the new phrase that described her, but the attention still made her uncomfortable. Still, it was better than *coward* or *fearful girl*.

She saw a group of Defiers walking toward the door and ran to meet them. Oliver, Sky, and Clover ran to her as she ran to them and they met in another relieved embrace.

"We made it!" Lennox looked at each one of their faces with a breath of victory.

They were finally safe.

Chapter 28

Soft, pink dandelions grew amongst the grass upon the hills of the hidden Sparrow City. Clover picked some and waved them in the air, making them float like fairies in the wind. Rosie sang praises so loud that her voice reached the heavens. The rest of the Defiers joined in on songs they knew. Their voices were not as smooth as hers, but it did not matter. Sheer joy exuded from their lips and made their songs a thing of beauty. Happiness was tangible. Everyone's face glowed with joy. It reminded Lennox of her mother's radiance in the vision she saw in the hospital. It was a light that came from within. It was so bright, Lennox was sure it did not matter how dark life got again, because their hope was greater than the darkness.

The expressions made as they passed through the steel-gray door were something captured by time. The door led to the underground city, but it did not look underground at all. Hundreds of cherry blossom trees lined the path they walked. Lennox's jaw dropped as her eyes beheld the tunnel the cherry blossoms created. Their branches grew into one another, creating a canopy. Light pink petals that flirted with white floated above their heads like snowflakes. Lennox reached out for one, but her hand brushed through it. The trees were holograms.

Oliver saw Lennox look at her hand where the petal's image fizzled away.

"We keep holograms up to remind us that the world was meant to be a beautiful place, and it helps keep the little ones entertained," he explained.

Lennox saw children playing under the holograms, chasing the petals that fell. Holograms or not, the trees were beautiful.

Sky and Clover looked at her with smiles that made their cheeks rise. Lennox was sure their faces mirrored her own. Sparrow City was a place that exceeded expectations. They had anticipated a city of refuge, but what they saw was beautiful. People of different races and backgrounds came together as a united front in the name of Christ. They were brought together by war, but held together by God's love, and it made Lennox feel empowered and free.

Oliver pointed to a narrow path. "Fresh water is down that way."

Lennox heard the sound of trickling water as they walked farther into the tunnel. The hills had an aquifer that flowed freely underneath them.

Oliver continued to lead them down into the city and showed them the Sparrow training facilities. Lennox knew that was where she wanted to be and pulled Oliver aside.

"How do I become a Sparrow?" she asked, not wanting to waste a second.

She could not stay underground and hide when there were still people imprisoned. Sky joined her and asked the same question. She looked at him with empathy.

Oliver shook his head and walked a little farther with Sky and Lennox following close behind.

"You make a vow on Confirmation Day, and then you train." Oliver nodded to the room that was divided from the rest of the underground city.

"Then that's what I am going to do," Lennox said, knowing that her mom and dad would be proud of who they had become. She would continue what her parents started and would become a part of the legacy. She would get the locket back and fight for others.

Oliver gave Lennox a hug, "Mom and Dad would be proud of you."

"Of us," Lennox said, bumping into him and continued, "Thank you for fighting and always being there for me."

"That is what I am here for," Oliver said, throwing his arm over Lennox's shoulders.

She knew the life of a Sparrow would not be easy, but it would be worth it. There was still so much more that had to be done.

The day came. It was Confirmation Day.

Everything she had been through led her to this moment. She was not entirely who she wanted to be, but she was for sure not who she used to be. She was no longer someone who ran away, controlled by fear. The *D* on her arm was her new identity—not just a label the Regime branded her with. Every single day there was a war that must be fought, and she would fight it. She lived, moved, and had her being to serve the Lord and defy the Regime.

The underground arena was filled with hundreds of

men and women who chose to fight the good fight of faith. Lennox would soon be one of them. Their Sparrow uniforms made the stands a sea of gray and red. Lennox could not help but admire it. The circular front stage was set for the vow ceremony.

She stood on black granite behind the crimson curtain, waiting for her name to be called. She had butterflies soaring in circles in her stomach. She lifted herself on her tip-toes and rocked back on her heels. She inhaled deeply and exhaled slowly as she waited.

Lennox watched Sky appear from behind the curtain as his name was called. He took one last glance at her and smiled, making his dimples bury into his cheeks. Lennox shook her head and smiled back. Peeking out from behind the curtain, she watched as Sky made his vow. A loud roar followed. Clover sat in the front row, cheering the loudest with her young voice.

Then the orator called her name.

"Lennox Winters."

She stepped out from behind the curtain where stone pillars with flames towered around her. She straightened her posture as everyone cheered and stood to their feet. Sweat filled her palms as she made her way to the orator. She raised her right hand and placed her left hand on the

Bible the orator held.

Faith was a reason to fight. She realized that now. She wanted to be a part of something bigger than herself.

She made her vow.

"I, Lennox Grace Winters, do solemnly vow that I will support and defend the cause of Christ against all enemies, and I will bear true faith and allegiance to the Lord Almighty. I acknowledge His sovereignty, and will give Him glory all the days of my life, until the last breath."

The orator handed her a Sparrow uniform. Two Sparrows standing at the bottom of the stage lifted trumpets to their mouths and sounded the charge. Shouts of victory filled Lennox's ears. She shouted the war cry with the crowd. The Lord was on her side, and He had never asked her to go to war without Him. There was no turning back.

One way or another, through life or through death, victory was hers.

Chapter 29

It was the first day of Sparrow training and Lennox was ready to learn. She stood in the locker room of the training facility and put her old clothes in the red lockers that lined the jagged, stone walls. Her heart raced as she put on the steel-gray Sparrow jumpsuit. As she zipped it up, she placed her pointer finger on the sleeve's embroidery and traced its sparrow outline. The fabric was thick and tough, yet still soft to the touch.

Her mind thought about how God's perfect love casts out all fear. She remembered that Jesus had already conquered death, hell, and the grave. Death lost its sting, and the grave no longer had victory over those who believed... and *she* believed. There was nothing truer to her than her faith. Every bit of hell she had been through was worth it all.

She walked into the hall of the training facility and waited for Sky to exit the men's makeshift locker room.

He stepped out and she smiled at how handsome he looked. Oliver walked out behind him and motioned for them to come forward.

"Y'all ready?" he asked as he led them to the hollowed out cave .

Sparrows in full combat scenarios fought holograms of Regime soldiers. Easton came to greet them as they stood by the opening. Her black hair was pulled in a tight bun that pulled her face in a harsh way, but the sharp lines of her face could not disguise the light that came from her eyes.

Oliver introduced her, "This is Instructor Easton. She is one of the best."

Easton extended her hand to Sky.

"I'm Sky, nice to meet you." He shook her hand.

"Nice to meet you," she replied.

"And you know my sister, Lennox," Oliver said, pointing to Lennox.

Lennox smiled and shook Easton's hand. "Nice to see you again."

Easton smiled. "Let's see what your natural instincts are."

She handed them Sapphire Shields and two firearms that looked similar to ones the Sparrows used at the outpost. The glowing, blue ammunition showed through the barrel.

"These guns do not bring death, but judgment," she continued, "The blue liquid delivers the same pain the recipient has caused others. It immobilizes them so that we can put them in prison where they belong."

Easton pointed them to an open mat. Sky and Lennox stepped onto it and holograms immediately charged toward them. Hologram bullets flew in front of their faces and Lennox lifted her shield to block them. The images of the bullets disappeared when they hit. Regime soldiers came closer. Sky drew his gun and fired. The holograms fell to their knees and vanished.

Easton stepped onto the mat. "Both of you have good instincts. Six months of training and you will be ready for the field."

Sky and Lennox looked at each other with wide eyes. They never thought their lives would turn out this way, but they had. They wanted to serve. It was their mission to rescue all who were imprisoned.

Lennox resolved to not be less than what she was—a soldier in the Lord's army.

A Sparrow.

God's plan was her destiny. Stronger, wiser, and

braver was what she aspired to, and she would be… for Christ. She finally realized that life was more than flesh and bone. Faith in Christ had turned her fate around. Her life's meaning was only found when she fought for what she believed in.

Her training was only the beginning of her new journey. She would train her hardest. She knew that Sparrow City would not stay underground for much longer. She knew a day would come when the city was no longer hidden behind the hills, but would sit upon them as a beacon of light to all who dare to defy. With God before her and fear behind her, she would do as her parents instructed her to do. There was a reason she still stood. She would get the locket back, and she would fulfill her purpose.

She would *fight*.

Acknowledgements

I want to give thanks to my Lord and Savior, Jesus Christ. He has never failed me and has always given me a reason to stand. Lord, thank you for loving me despite all of my failures. Thank you for turning my fear into faith. Thank you for the cross!

Thank you to my loving and supportive husband, Brandon, who encourages and inspires me. You have taught me how to be bold for Christ. And thank you to my children, Ty and J, may you be brave for Christ no matter what. I love all three of you more than words can express!

Mom and Dad, thank you for believing in me from the start. Mom, thank you for encouraging me to seek the Lord in the process of writing this novel and for believing in my dream from the first draft. Dad, thank you for the help with the tech and science fiction elements. I love you both very much!

Huge thanks to my friend and fellow writer, Veronica

Lynn, who became my developmental editor and helped me to pick apart every draft to see what worked and what didn't. You have been a true blessing through the whole process - story boarding and all. My words will never be enough to express my gratefulness for the time you have spent on this project with me.

Thank you so much to Mr. Mitchell, who so graciously helped to polish the manuscript. You deserve an award for taking Defier out of the mire and making it shine.

Thank you to my church family and Pastors who have always supported my writing endeavors. I am beyond blessed to be a part of one of the greatest church families I have ever seen.

To my fellow Christian authors, who took the time to inspire and reach out to a new author, thank you for your kindness and grace. Your words of experience helped me more than you'll ever know.

Last, but certainly not least, thank you to all of my beta readers and readers who have given Defier a chance. Without you, a part of my dream would not come true. With you, my dream has come alive! THANK YOU!!!

You all are a blessing!

Want more DEFIER?

Check for news and updates on:

 @mandyfender11

 Mandy Fender Author Page

To see the DEFIER playlist go to:

mandyfender.com

AND DON'T MISS

DEFIER SERIES BOOK TWO
Available Summer 2016

About the Author

Mandy Fender lives in the great state of Texas with her family and bulldog. Some of her favorite things include spending time with her family, reading, and playing sports.

She has served in youth ministry for over ten years and loves to hear testimonies concerning what God is doing in young people.